Charles H. Grandgent

Italian Grammar

Charles H. Grandgent

Italian Grammar

ISBN/EAN: 9783337238667

Printed in Europe, USA, Canada, Australia, Japan

Cover: Foto ©Andreas Hilbeck / pixelio.de

More available books at **www.hansebooks.com**

ITALIAN GRAMMAR.

BY

C. H. GRANDGENT,

TUTOR IN MODERN LANGUAGES IN HARVARD UNIVERSITY.

BOSTON: U.S.A.

D. C. HEATH & CO., PUBLISHERS,

1889.

PREFACE.

THIS volume is the result of an attempt to put into convenient form and the smallest possible compass all the grammar that the ordinary student of Italian will need. Short as the book is, it contains some paragraphs which beginners will probably skip : the longer lists of words and endings, and a great part of the chapters on suffixes and irregular verbs will be useful mainly for reference. The vocabularies cover the twenty-one translation exercises, but not the examples nor the Exercise in Pronunciation ; they are not intended to include words explained in the notes, nor proper names that are exactly the same in Italian and in English.

I have endeavored to make the book represent the Italian language as it is spoken and written at the present day ; the exercises are taken chiefly from reading-books lately prepared for Tuscan schools. Still, I have tried to give also as many obsolete forms as students of the Italian classics will require.

It has been my aim throughout to make the rules clear for all classes of pupils, even for those ignorant of other foreign languages, provided they understand the technical words commonly used in grammars. With this object in view, I have ascribed to the Italian vowels the pronunciation of the English ones that are most like them : an accurate description of the Italian sounds would, I fear, prove confusing to beginners who have had no training in phonetics. It will be easy for the instructor to explain not only the vowels, but some of the consonants, and the division of words into syllables, much better than can be done in a book like this.

The authorities I have consulted most are the dictionaries of Fanfani, Rigutini and Fanfani, Fornari (*Nuovo Bazzarini*), and Tommaseo and Bellini. I have made but little use of other grammars; I am, however, indebted to Toscani for some ideas and a few of my examples. The chapters on syntax, and the treatment of irregular verbs, pronouns, suffixes, and the plural of words in -*co* and -*go* are almost entirely the result of original work.

In conclusion, I wish to express my gratitude to Professor Nash, of Harvard, to my friend and teacher, Sig. Filippo Orlando, of Florence, and to the gentlemen who assisted me in correcting the proof-sheets; and I wish above all to thank Professor Sheldon, of Harvard, and Professor Bendelari, of Yale, without whose aid and encouragement I should scarcely have ventured to offer this book to the public.

CAMBRIDGE, September, 1887.

TABLE OF CONTENTS.

ITALIAN GRAMMAR.

PRONUNCIATION.

1. In Italian all the letters are pronounced, except *h*, which is always silent. *B, f, g, l, m, n, p, q, s,* and *v* are pronounced as in English. The letters of the Italian alphabet are named as follows : —

A, *ah.*	G, *jē.*	N, *èn-nĕ.*	T, *tē.*
B, *bē.*	H, *ák-kah.*	O, *ŏ.*	U, *oo.*
C, *chē.*	I, *ē.*	P, *pē.*	V, *vē.*
D, *dē.*	J, *ē loongo.*	Q, *coo.*	Z, *dzē-tah.*
E, *ā.*	L, *èl-lĕ.*	R, *èr-rĕ.*	
F, *èf-fĕ.*	M, *èm-mĕ.*	S, *ès-sĕ.*	

In the italicized words above, the letters and signs have their English values; the accented syllable is marked by an acute accent (′).

2. A is always pronounced like *a* in English "father": as *fáma*, "fame."

I is always pronounced like *e* in "he": as *víni*, "wines."

U always has the sound of *oo* in "moon": as *úna*, "one."

Even when these vowels are short their quality remains unchanged: as *pálla*, "ball"; *spílli*, "pins"; *núlla*, "nothing."

a. In the groups *cia, cio, ciu, gia, gio, giu,* the *i*, unless it be accented, is generally not pronounced ; it is merely a graphic sign, denoting that the *c* or the *g* is soft. Soft *c* is like English *ch* in "chin"; soft *g* is like *g* in "gem." Ex.: *ciò*, "that"; *guáncia*, "cheek"; *mángia*, "he eats"; *giù*, "down."

3. E has two sounds : one close, like *a* in "gate," one open, like *e* in "get." Unaccented *e* is always close. The cases where accented *e* is open and those where it is close must be learned by practice ;* but in the group *ie* it is always open. In this book an acute accent (´) marks the close, and a circumflex (ˆ) the open sound ; these accents are, however, not used in writing Italian. Ex.: *spésso*, "often"; *védo*, "I see"; *êbbe*, "he had"; *viêne*, "he comes."

O has also two sounds : one close, like *o* in "note," one open, like *o* in "for."† Unaccented *o* is always close. In the group *uo*, accented *o* is always open. Ex.: *pómo*, "fruit"; *mólto*, "much"; *pôco*, "little"; *fuôco*, "fire."

a. The groups *ie* and *uo* nearly always form but one syllable each, the accent being on the *e* and the *o* : as *piêno*, "full"; *buôno*, "good."

b. In the suffixes *-eccio* (*-a*), *-esco* (*-a*), *-ese, -essa, -etto* (*-a*), *-ezzo* (*-a*), *-mente*, and *-mento* the *e* is always close ; while in the diminutive suffix *-ello* (*-a*), and in the endings *-ente, -enza, -erio* (or *-ero*), and *-esimo* (*-a*) it is open : as *inglése*, "English"; *probabilménte*, "probably"; *prudênte*, "prudent"; *ventêsimo*, "twentieth."

---

* Italian *e* is close when it represents Latin *ē* or *ĭ*; open when it represents Latin *ĕ* or *ae*. This rule has very few exceptions.

† Italian *o* is close when it represents Latin *ō* or *ŭ*; open when it represents Latin *ŏ* or *au*.

c. In the endings *-oio, -one, -ore,* and in the suffix *-oso* (*-a*) the *o* is close; while in the ending *-orio,* and in *-occio* (*-a*), *-otto* (*-a*), and *-ozzo* (*-a*), used as suffixes to nouns or adjectives, it is open: as *vassóio,* "tray"; *amóre,* "love"; *romitório,* "hermitage"; *casótta,* "good-sized house."

d. In poetry and in some prose *o* is often used instead of *uo*; this *o* is always open: as *córe* (for *cuóre*), "heart."

4. **C** before *a, o, u,* or a consonant is pronounced like English *k*: as *cása,* "house." Before *e* or *i* it has the value of *ch* in "chin":* as *dólce,* "sweet"; *cínque,* "five."

When double *c* precedes *e* or *i,* both *c*'s are soft: as *fáccia,* "face."

G before *a, o, u,* or a consonant is pronounced as in English: as *gátto,* "cat." Before *e* or *i* it has the value of *g* in "gem":* as *gênte,* "people"; *giórno,* "day."

When double *g* precedes *e* or *i,* both *g*'s are soft; as *rággio,* "ray."

H is always silent: as *ha,* "he has."
J is merely another way of writing *i* or *ii.*
R is always rolled: as *cárne,* "meat"; *rósso,* "red"; *per,* "for." When *r* is double, the trill is prolonged: as *búrro,* "butter"; *marróne,* "chestnut."
S is generally like English *s* in "see," "mason": as *sô,* "I know"; *cása,* "house"; *diségno,* "design." But a single *s* between two vowels is very often sounded like English *z*: as *cáso,* "case"; *disonóre,* "dishonor."

---

* Between two vowels, of which the second is *e* or *i,* single *c* and single *g* are, in Tuscany, pronounced respectively like *sh* in "shin," and like *si* in "vision" (French *g* in *page*): as *páce,* "peace"; *stagióne,* "season."

In the suffixes *-ése* and *-ésimo* the *s* is sounded *z*; in the suffix *-óso* it is like *s* in "mason"; as *francése*, "French"; *noióso*, "troublesome."

Initial *s*, followed by *b, d, g, l, m, n,* or *v,* is pronounced *z*: as *sdruccioláre*, "to slip"; *slítta*, "sleigh."

T and d are pronounced further forward in the mouth than in English; the tip of the tongue should touch the back of the upper front teeth: as *tu*, "thou"; *féde*, "faith."

z is sounded like *ts*: as *alzáre*, "to lift." After *n*, however, *z* is, in many words, pronounced *dz*: as *mánzo*, "beef"; *zanzára*, "mosquito." At the beginning of a word *z* always has the sound of *dz* (as *zínco*, "zinc"), except in *zámpa, zía, zío, zítto, zólfo, zóppo, zúcca, zúcchero, zúppa,* and some other words that are but little used.*

Zz is sometimes *tts*, sometimes *ddz*:† as *prézzo (tts),* "price"; *mézzo (ddz),* "half."

---

* The complete list is: —

zabattiêro	zána	zázzera	zíngaro	zôlfa
zaccágna	zánca	zécca	zinghináia	zólfo
záccaro	zángola	zéppa	zinzíno	zombáre
zácchera	zánna	zéppo	zío	zôppo
záffo	zánni	zighêna	zípolo	zúcca
zambúco	zánza	zígolo	zitêllo	zúcchero
zámpa	záppa	zimár	zítto	záffa
zampíllo	zátta	zimbêllo	zívolo	zúfolo
zampógna	zazzeáre	zinfonía	zôcco	zúppa

and their derivatives.

† In general *zz* is *tts* when it comes from Latin *ti, ddz* when it comes from Latin *di*: as *pretium = prézzo; medium = mézzo.*

In the suffixes -*ázzo* (-*a*), -*ézzo* (-*a*), -*ízzo* (-*a*), -*ózzo* (-*a*), and -*úzzo* (-*a*) the *zz* is sounded *tts*, but in the verbal ending -*izzáre* it is *ddz* : as *chiarézza*, "clearness" ; *utilizzáre*, "to utilize."

The other consonants are pronounced as in English.

5. The following combinations are to be noted : —

Cb (which is used only before *e* and *i*) is always like English *k*: as *fíchi*, "figs." **Sch** is like *sk*: as *schérzo*, "sport."

Gh (which is used only before *e* and *i*) is always like English *g* in "get" : as *ághi*, "needles."

Gli (written *gl* if the following vowel be *i*) is like English *lli* in "million" : * as *fíglio*, "son" ; *fígli*, "sons."

Gn is like *ni* in "onion" : as *bisógno*, "need."

Gu followed by a vowel is like *gw*: as *guáncia*, "cheek."

Qu is always like *kw* : as *quésto*, "this."

Sc before *e* and *i* is like *sh* in "shin" : as *uscíre*, "to go out." Before all other letters it is pronounced *sk*: as *scuóla*, "school."

6. With the exception of *h* and of the combinations mentioned in **5** and in **2,** *a*, every letter in Italian is distinctly sounded. In pronouncing double consonants both letters must be sounded — the first at the end of the preceding, the second at the beginning of the following syllable. Ex. : *paura* (*pa-ú-ra*), "fear" ; *Europa* (*E-u-rô-pa*), "Europe" ; *miei* (*miê-i*), "my" ; *babbo* (*báb-bo*), "papa" ; *fatto* (*fát-to*), "done" ; *anno* (*án-no*), "year" ; *fáccia* (pronounce *fat-tsha*), "face" ; *ôggi* (pronounce *od-dgê*), "today" ; *pázzo* (pronounce *pat-tso*), "mad."

---

* Exceptions are *negligere*, and a few uncommon words borrowed from the Latin ; in these *gl* = English *gl*.

7. In writing Italian only one accent, the grave ('), is employed.* Any vowel bearing this mark is accented and (if it be *e* or *o*) open in the pronunciation. When, as is the case with nearly all words, no accent is written, the emphasized syllable must be learned by practice.† Most nouns and adjectives are accented on the penult. In this book the accent will always be marked.

8. Italian words are divided into syllables in such a way that, if possible, every syllable begins with a consonant : as *ta-vo-lí-no*, "table." When *s* precedes another consonant, both that consonant and the *s* belong to the following syllable : as *di-stán-te*, "distant"; *ri-strét-to*, "limited." When *r* follows another consonant, both that consonant and the *r* belong to the following syllable : as *pá-dre*, "father"; *a-vrò*, "I shall have." Ex. : *mi-glió-re*, "better"; *o-gnú-no*, "every"; *ri-spón-de-re*, "to reply"; *te-á-tro*, "theatre"; *del-l' ác-qua*, "of the water."

EXERCISE IN PRONUNCIATION.

Carlíno è maláto, è mólto maláto. Lì da lúi al súo letticciuôlo,
Charley is   ill   is very   ill   There by him at(the) his   little-bed

c' è sêmpre la mámma. La mámma è sêmpre li, è sêmpre li
there is always the mother   The mother is always there is always there

giórno e nôtte. È ôtto giórni che non si è spogliáta ; quándo
day and night   It-is eight days that not she-has-undressed when

non ne può più, appôggia il cápo accánto al visíno del
she-cannot(-hold-out) more she-leans the head beside (to)the little-face of (the)

súo Carlíno, e s' appísola un pôco : ma dormíre, ah ! dormíre non
her Charley and drowses a little but sleep ah sleep not

---

* Some Italian authors and editors use the acute and circumflex accents to mark proparoxytones, and to distinguish words that are alike in spelling but different in meaning; but their example is not generally followed.

† The accent is nearly always the same as in Latin.

può. Che se Carlíno tósse, se álza úna manína, se respíra un
she-can For if Charley coughs if he-raises a little-hand if he-breathes a

po' più fòrte, la mámma è súbito alzáta, e lo guárda físso
little more hard the mother is at-once arisen and him looks-at hard

físso, e lo bácia. Il malatíno patísce, ma patísce più la póvera
hard and him kisses The little-invalid suffers but suffers more the poor

mámma.
mother.

_____

ARTICLES.

9. The article is not declined, but it agrees with its substantive in gender and number.

THE DEFINITE ARTICLE.

10. Masculine :—

a. Sing. *il*, pl. *i*, before a word beginning with any consonant except *s* impure* and *z*.

b. Sing. *lo*, pl. *gli*, before a word beginning with a vowel or with *s* impure or *z*.

Before a vowel *lo* becomes *l'*; *gli* becomes *gl'* before *i*.

Ex.: *Il pádre*, the father ; *i pádri*, the fathers.
Lo stésso pádre, the same father.
Lo scidme, the swarm ; *gli scidmi*, the swarms.
Lo zio, the uncle ; *gli zii*, the uncles.
L' uómo, the man ; *gl' insétti*, the insects.

11. Feminine :—

Sing. *la*, pl. *le*.

Before a vowel *la* becomes *l'*; *le* becomes *l'* before *e*.

Ex.: *La mádre*, the mother ; *le mádri*, the mothers.
L' óra, the hour ; *le óre*, the hours ; *l' érbe*, the herbs.

_____

* That is, *s* followed by another consonant.

12. When the definite article is preceded by one of the prepositions *di, da, a, in, con, su, per,* the article and preposition are generally contracted into one word, as shown in the following table (*con, per,* are often uncontracted) : —

	IL	I	LO	GLI	LA	LE	L'
Di, of	del	*dèi* or *de'*	*dèllo*	*dègli*	*dèlla*	*dèlle*	*dell'*
Da, by	dal	*dài* or *da'*	*dàllo*	*dàgli*	*dàlla*	*dàlle*	*dall'*
A, to	al	*ài* or *a'*	*àllo*	*àgli*	*àlla*	*àlle*	*all'*
In, in	nel	*nèi* or *ne'*	*nèllo*	*nègli*	*nèlla*	*nèlle*	*nell'*
Con, with	col	*còi* or *co'*	*còllo*	*cògli*	*còlla*	*còlle*	*coll'*
Su, on	sul	*sùi* or *su'*	*sùllo*	*sùgli*	*sùlla*	*sùlle*	*sull'*
Per, for	pel	*pèi* or *pe'*	per lo	per gli	per la	per le	per l'

Ex.: *Del pàdre*, of the father; *dài pàdri*, by the fathers.
Àllo spêcchio, to the mirror; *nègli spêcchi*, in the mirrors.
Còlla màdre, with the mother; *còlle màdri*, with the mothers.
Sull' uômo, on the man; *per gli uômini*, for the men.

a. The word "some" is frequently rendered in Italian by *di* with the definite article. This is called the partitive genitive.

Ex.: *Dátemi del vino*, give me some wine.
Délle bèlle còse, some fine things.

13. In the following cases the definite article is used in Italian, though not in English : —

a. Before the possessive pronouns : as *il nòstro giardino*, "our garden"; *i suôi fratêlli*, "his brothers." When, however, the possessive qualifies an otherwise unmodified noun in the singular expressing relationship, the article is generally omitted: as *mia màdre*, "my mother." For a fuller statement see **45**, *a.*

b. Before an abstract noun or one denoting a whole class.

Ex.: *L' uômo propône*, man proposes.
I fiôri nâscono dal séme, flowers spring from the seed.
Gli uccêlli hânno le âli, birds have wings.
La môrte è il peggiôre di tútti i mâli, death is the worst of all
evils.

c. In general before a noun used with any adjective that does
not express quantity.

Ex.: *L'ânno scórso*, last year.
Gli uômini buôni, good men.
Il pôvero Giôrgio non viêne, poor George doesn't come.

d. Before a title followed by a proper name.

Ex.: *La regîna Vittôria*, Queen Victoria.
Il signór Áscoli, Mr. Ascoli.

e. Before family names; often before given names of women;
occasionally before given names of well-known men.

Ex.: *Il Biânchi è môrto*, White is dead; *la Pâtti cânta*, Patti sings.
Conôsco l' Olîvia, I know Olivia.
Il poèma del Dânte or *di Dânte*, Dante's poem.

f. (1) Before names of countries and continents.

Ex.: *La Svizzera*, Switzerland; *all' Itâlia*, to Italy.
Per l' Eurôpa, for Europe.

(2) But the article is omitted after *in*, in phrases that denote
going to or dwelling in a country.

Ex.: *Vâdo in Germânia*, I go to Germany.
Rimângo in Frância, I remain in France.

(3) It is often omitted also after *di*, when *di* with the name of
a country is equivalent to an adjective of nationality.

Ex.: *La regina d' Inghiltèrra*, the queen of England.
Il vino di Spâgna, the wine of Spain.

In all the above cases (beginning with **13, a**) the article
is omitted if the noun is used as a vocative, or is modified
by a numeral or a pronominal adjective.

Ex.: *Viéni, amico mìo*, come, my friend.
Quésta sùa ópera, this work of his.
Vi sóno sétte virtù, there are seven virtues.
Póvero pádre, poor father!
Dùe bellissimi cáni, two very beautiful dogs.
Signóra Mónti, cóme sta, Mrs. Monti, how do you do?
Itália, ti rivédo, Italy, I see thee again.

THE INDEFINITE ARTICLE.

14. Masculine:—

a. *Un* before a vowel or any consonant except *s* impure and *z*.
b. *Úno* before *s* impure or *z*.

Ex.: *Un pádre*, a father; *un uómo*, a man.
Un anéllo, a ring; *úno spécchio*, a mirror.
Úno sciáme, a swarm; *úno zío*, an uncle.

15. Feminine:—

Úna, which becomes *un'* before a vowel.

Ex.: *Úna mádre*, a mother; *un' óra*, an hour.

16. In the following cases the indefinite article, though expressed in English, is omitted in Italian:—

a. Before a predicate noun expressing occupation, rank, or nationality, and not accompanied by an adjective.

Ex.: *Égli è poéta*, he is a poet; *sóno marchése*, I am a marquis.
Siéte italiáno, you are an Italian.

b. Generally before an antecedent (of a relative clause) used in apposition to a preceding noun modified by a definite article or a demonstrative pronoun.

Ex.: *L' Árno, fiùme che travérsa Firènze*, the Arno, a river which traverses Florence.

EXERCISE I.

La párte più álta del nôstro córpo è il cápo. Il cápo è attaccáto
highest *is* *is attached*
al côllo, e il côllo è attaccáto al trónco. La párte davánti del
front
cápo si chiáma víso. Nel víso ci sóno la frônte, gli ôcchi, il
is-called *there are* *eyes*
náso, la bócca, il ménto. Cógli ôcchi si védono le côse. Col
we-see *things*
náso si sêntono gli odóri. Cólla bócca si mángia, si béve, si
we-smell *odors* *we-eat* *we-drink we-*
respíra. Respiráre è mandáre l'ária giù nel pêtto, e pôi riman-
breathe
dárla fuôri. Nói respiriámo l'ária. Leváte un pésce dall'ácqua,
it *We breathe* *Take*
muôre : leváte l'ária a nói, e nói morrémo.
it-dies *take* *from us* *shall-die.*

EXERCISE 2.

Mr. Rossi is a merchant. Leaving Italy, he-went-away last
è *Lasciándo* *partì*
year to France, a country which he-wished to-visit with his brother
per *voléva* *visitáre*
and a friend of the family. But he-returned to Italy the same
tornò *in*
month, saying : "Travelling[1] bores-me. Another time I-shall-make
dicêndo *viaggiáre (m.)* *mi sécca* *Un' áltra* *farò*
a study of the customs of France. Paris is a big city ; we-have-
costúmi (m. pl.) *grànde* *vi abbiàmo*
seen some[2] fine things ; but I-prefer the land of Garibaldi and
vedúto *bélle côse(f. pl.)* *mi piáce più*
of King Victor Emmanuel."

[1] See 13, b. [2] See 12, a.

NOUNS.

17. Italian nouns are not declined. Possession is de-
noted by the preposition *di :* as *lo spécchio di mío pádre,*
"my father's looking-glass."

GENDER.

18. There are no neuter nouns in Italian.*

Nouns denoting males and females keep their natural gender, whatever their termination may be : except *guída*, "guide"; *guárdia*, "guard"; *sentinélla*, "sentinel"; *spía*, "spy"; which are feminine.

> Ex.: *Il fratéllo*, the brother; *mía sorélla*, my sister.
> *Il poéta*, the poet; *la poetéssa*, the poetess.
> *Úna spía*, a spy; *la nóstra guída*, our guide.

19. Of nouns denoting objects without sex some are masculine, some feminine. Their gender can often be determined by the final letter. All Italian nouns end in *a, e, i, o,* or *u* :† —

a. Those ending in *a* are feminine ; except *coléra*, "cholera," Greek neuters in *-ma*,‡ many geographical names, and a few other words, mostly foreign.

> Ex.: *Un' óra*, an hour ; *un telegrámma*, a telegram.
> *Il Canadá*, Canada ; *il sofà*, the sofa.

b. Of those ending in *e* and *i* some are masculine, some feminine. All ending in *-zióne*, *-gióne*, or *-údine* are feminine.

> Ex.: *Il fiúme*, the river : *la páce*. peace.
> *Un dì*, a day ; *una metrópoli*, a metropolis.
> *La ragióne*, the reason ; *la servitúdine*, service.

c. Those ending in *o* are masculine; except *máno*, "hand."

> Ex.: *Il ginócchio*, the knee ; *la máno*, the hand.

---

* Latin neuters become masculine in Italian ; masculines and feminines retain their Latin gender. This rule has very few exceptions.

† A few foreign nouns used in Italian end in a consonant : as *lápis*, "pencil."

‡ Mostly scientific terms.

d. Those ending in *u* are feminine; except *soprappiù*, "surplus," and a few foreign words.

Ex.: *La virtù*, virtue; *il bambù*, bamboo.

20. Any other part of speech (except an adjective*) used as a noun must be masculine.

Ex.: *Il viaggiáre*, travelling.

21. Masculine names of trees in *o* or *e* have a feminine form in *a* or *e* respectively, denoting their fruit; but *il dáttero*, "date," *il fíco*, "fig," *il limóne*, "lemon," *il pómo*, "apple," are always the same, whether denoting the tree or the fruit.

Ex.: *Un susíno*, a plum-tree; *una susína*, a plum.
Il nóce, the walnut-tree; *la nóce*, the walnut.
Quésti fíchi, these fig-trees, these figs.

NUMBER.

22. Feminines in unaccented *a* form their plural by changing *a* into *e*.

Ex.: *La stráda*, the street; *le stráde*, the streets.
Una bugía, a lie; *le bugíe*, lies.

a. Feminines in *-ca* and *-ga* form their plural in *-che* and *-ghe* respectively (the *h* being inserted merely to indicate that the *c* and *g* keep their hard sound).

Ex.: *Un' óca*, a goose; *mólte óche*, many geese.
La bottéga, the shop; *parécchie bottéghe*, several shops.

---

* Adjectives of course have the gender of the nouns they represent.

b. Nouns in unaccented *-cia* and *-gia* form their plural in *-ce* and *-ge* respectively.*

Ex.: *La guáncia*, the cheek; *le guánce*, the cheeks.
Úna ciliègia, a cherry; *tánte ciliège*, so many cherries.

23. Masculines in unaccented *a* and all nouns in unaccented *o* and *c* (not *ie*) form their plural in *i*.

Ex.: *Un poéta*, a poet; *dúe poéti*, two poets.
Lo zío, the uncle; *gli zii*, the uncles.
La máno, the hand; *le míe máni*, my hands.
Un mése, a month; *tre mési*, three months.
La corníce, the frame; *quáttro corníci*, four frames.

a. Masculines in *-ca* and *-ga* form their plural in *-chi* and *-ghi* respectively.

Ex.: *Il monárca*, the monarch; *i monárchi*, the monarchs.
Il collèga, the colleague; *i collèghi*, the colleagues.

b. Nouns in unaccented *-io* form their plural by changing *-io* to *-i* (often written *ii* or *j*).

Ex.: *Lo spècchio*, the mirror; *gli spècchi*, the mirrors.
Il ciliègio, the cherry-tree; *i ciliègi*, the cherry-trees.

c. Nouns in *-go* form their plural in *-ghi*. Nouns in *-co* form their plural in *-chi* if the penult is accented, otherwise in *-ci*.

Ex.: *Il castígo*, the punishment; *i castíghi*, the punishments.
Un catálogo, a catalogue; *dúe catáloghi*, two catalogues.
Il fíco, the fig; *cínque fíchi*, five figs.
Antíco, ancient; *gli antíchi*, the ancients.
Un mèdico, a doctor; *sèi mèdici*, six doctors.

This rule has a number of exceptions. In the following lists, words whose irregular plural is rare are omitted.

---

* A few nouns in unaccented *-cia* and *-gia* are commonly written with the *i* in the plural: as *alterigia* (*alterigie*), *audácia* (*-cie*), *cupidigia* (*-gie*), *fallácia* (*-cie*), *feròcia* (*-cie*), *provincia* (*-cie*).

(1) When *mágo*, "magician," means "one of the Magi," its plural is *mági;* otherwise it is *mághi*. Compound nouns in *-logo* denoting persons engaged in the sciences form their plural in *-gi*. Compound nouns in *-fago* form their plural in *-gi*.*

Ex.: *Il fisiólogo*, the physiologist; *i fisiólogi*, physiologists.
Antropófago, cannibal; *antropófagi*, cannibals.

(2) The following words form their plural in *-ci*, although the penult is accented : —

| amíco | grêco | inimíco | nemíco | pôrco † |

Grêco has a regular plural in the expression *vini grêchi*.

(3) The following words form their plural in *-chi*, although the penult is unaccented : —

ábbaco	fármaco	lástrico	rammárico	stráscico
acróstico	índaco	mánico	rísico	tôssico
cárico ‡	intônaco	párroco	sciático	tráffico
diméntico ‡	intrínseco	pízzico	stômaco	válico §

Acróstico and *fármaco* have also regular plurals.

d. Some masculines in *o* have an irregular plural in *a*; this plural is feminine. They are : *centinádio*, "hundred"; *migliáio*, "thousand"; *miglio*, "mile"; *páio*, "pair"; *uôvo*, "egg."

Many masculines in *o* have this irregular feminine plural in *a* besides the regular masculine plural in *i*. The most common are : *bráccio*, "arm"; *díto*, "finger"; *frútto*, "fruit"; *ginôcchio*, "knee"; *grído*, "shout"; *lábbro*, "lip"; *légno*, "wood"; *mêmbro*, "member"; *múro*, "wall"; *orécchio*, "ear"; *ôsso*, "bone."

---

* Likewise the rare or obsolete words: *flemmagógo, idragógo, metallúrgo, sárgo* (also reg. plur.), *sortilego*.

† Likewise the rare words: *aprico, lombrico* (also reg.), *uvamíco, vico*.

‡ Likewise its compounds.

§ Likewise the rare or obsolete words: *fildccico, mántaco* (also reg.), *ostático, sfiláccico, stático* (noun), *úncico*.

Ex. : *Un páio,* a pair ; *sètte páia,* seven pairs.
Il mío bráccio, my arm ; *le túe bráccia,* thy arms.
Il lábbro, the lip ; *le lábbra* or *i lábbri,* the lips.
Un ôsso, a bone ; *le óssa* or *gli óssi,* the bones.

Bráccio, ginôcchio, lábbro, and *orécchio* nearly always have the irregular plural when denoting the two arms, knees, lips, or ears belonging to the same body.

24. All monosyllables, and all nouns ending in *i, ie, u,* an accented vowel, or a consonant, are invariable.

Ex. : *Il re,* the king ; *i re,* the kings.
Il bríndisi, the toast ; *i bríndisi,* the toasts.
Úna spècie. a kind ; *ôtto spècie,* eight kinds.
La virtù, virtue ; *le virtù,* the virtues.
Úna città, a city ; *dièci città,* ten cities.

25. The following nouns have irregular plurals : *búe,* "ox," pl. *buôi; dío,* "god," pl. *dèi*; *móglie,* "wife," pl. *mógli; uômo,* "man," pl. *uômini.*

EXERCISE 3.

Gli uccèlli, le farfálle, i pésci, il cáne, il mício, le lucêrtole sóno[1] tútti animáli. Il gátto e il cáne sóno[1] animáli che hánno[2] quáttro gámbe, hánno[3] quáttro piêdi, e però si chiámano[4] quadrúpedi. Il leóne è[1] il più bêllo e il più maestóso déi quadrúpedi. Gli uccêlli hánno[2] dúe zámpe ; ed hánno[3] le áli e con le áli vólano.[5] Ánche le farfálle hánno[2] le áli, ánche le ápi hánno[2] le áli, e vólano.[5] Le mósche, le zanzáre, le vêspe, e pôi mólti áltri animalíni, símili a quésti, si chiámano[4] insêtti. Gli uccêlli e gl' insêtti náscono[6] dálle uôva. Tútti quésti animáli vívono[7] in mêzzo all' ária. I pésci vívono[7] in mêzzo all' ácqua. I pésci non hánno[2] gámbe ; hánno[3] dálle párti quéllc alettíne ; e con quéste píccole

---

* The article used with *dèi* is *gli : gli dèi.*

alétte e con la códa nuôtano[8] e guízzan[9] via nell' ácqua, lêsti lêsti cóme un lámpo. Quélle alétte si chiámano[4] pínne. Le lucêrtole stríscian[11] su' múri, hánno[3] délle zampíne, ma rasênti rasênti al côrpo, e quándo si muôvono[10] ánche súlla têrra, strísciano.[11] Le sêrpi non hánno[2] gámbe ; e quésti animáli che non hánno[2] gámbe e che strísciano[11] sulla têrra, cóme le lucêrtole e le sêrpi, si chiáman[4] rêttili.

[1] $\grave{E}$ = is; *sóno* = are.   [2] Have.   [3] They have.   [4] *Si chiámano* = are called.   [5] They fly.   [6] Are born.   [7] Live.   [8] They swim.   [9] Dart.   [10] *Si muôvono* = they move.   [11] Crawl, they crawl.

EXERCISE 4.[1]

Mignonettes are[2] born from the seed. The seed, placed under ground, has[3] sprouted ; from one side it-has[3] put-out[4] shoots, which have-spread-out[5] through[6] the ground, and from one side it-has[3] sent forth the stalk, the little-branches,[7] the leaves, and[9] the flowers. Like mignonettes,[8] many other plants, herbs, and[9] flowers spring[10] from the seed. Flowers, herbs, grain, and trees are-called[11] vegetables. Vegetables have[3] roots, trunk, branches, twigs, leaves, flowers, and[9] fruit. Plants first produce[12] the flower and then the fruit. The trunk or stalk of plants is[2] that[13] which rests[14] on the roots and[15] comes[16] out from the ground ;[17] it-is-covered[18] with[19] branches and with[19] leaves. Of the stalk of plants, — for instance, of the trunk of trees, — we-make-use[20] for many purposes ; we-make[21] furniture, doors, windows, the beams that support[22] ceilings, ships, carriages, and[9] cars. The branches of trees are-burned,[23] and give-us[24] fire. Vegetables in-order-to[25] live have[3] need of earth, of water, and[9] of light.

[1] See **13**, *b.*   [2] Is = *è*; are = *sóno.*   [3] Has, it has = *ha*; have = *hanno.*   [4] *Mésso.*   [5] *Si sóno distése.*   [6] *Fra.*   [7] *Ramicélli.*   [8] Insert "and so."   [9] Omit.   [10] *Náscono.*   [11] *Si chiámano.*   [12] *Fánno.*   [13] *Quéllo.*   [14] *Pósa.*   [15] Insert "which."   [16] *Viêne.*   [17] Insert "and."   [18] *Si ricuôpre.*   [19] *Di.*   [20] *Ci servidmo.*   [21] *Faccidmo.*   [22] *Rêggono.*   [23] *Si brúciano.*   [24] *Ci dánno.*   [25] *Per.*

ADJECTIVES.

26. Adjectives agree with their substantives in gender and number. An adjective modifying two nouns of different genders is generally put in the masculine plural.

Ex.: *Il gátto è pulíto*, the cat is neat; *stánze pulíte*, neat rooms.
Una cása e un giardíno bellíni, a pretty house and garden.

27. Numeral and pronominal adjectives and the commonest adjectives of size and quantity precede their nouns; adjectives of shape and material follow; *bèllo, buôno*, and adjectives whose use is prompted by emotion, generally precede. Otherwise, of the noun and adjective, the one that contains the chief idea comes last.

Ex.: *La secónda vólta*, the second time; *quésta vólta*, this time.
Tróppo páne, too much bread; *le grándi città*, great cities.
Quésta pálla rotónda, this round ball.
La buóna mádre, the good mother; *póver' uômo*, poor man!
La vóstra gentilíssima léttera, your kind *letter*.
È un uômo gentilíssimo, he is a *kind* man.

GENDER AND NUMBER

28. Adjectives ending in *o* are masculine, and form their feminine in *a*. Adjectives in *e* are invariable in the singular.

Ex.: *Buôno stivalétto,* good boot; *buóna scárpa*, good shoe.
Ragázzo felíce, happy boy; *ragázza felíce*, happy girl.

29. Adjectives form their plural in the same way as nouns (see **22, 23**).

Ex.: *Sèi buôni cassettóni,* six good bureaus; *ôtto buóne séggiole*, eight good chairs.
Due uômini felíci, two happy men; *tre dònne felíci*, three happy women.

a. Parécchi, "several," has for its feminine *parécchie.*

Ex.: *Parécchi tavolini,* several tables; *parécchie tàvole,* several dinner-tables.

b. Quálche, "some," is used only in the singular, even when the meaning is plural.

Ex.: *Qudlche vólta,* sometimes.

c. When preceding a noun, *béllo,* "beautiful," has forms similar to those of the definite article; and *Sánto,* "Saint," and *gránde,* "great," have corresponding forms in the singular. *Buóno,* "good," when preceding its noun, has a singular similar to the indefinite article. The masculine of these words (which is the only irregular part) is, therefore, as follows: —

Before any consonant except *s* impure or *z*: *bel, San, gran, buon;* pl. *béi, Sánti, grándi, buóni.*

Before *s* impure or *z*: *béllo, Sánto, gránde, buóno;* pl. *bégli, Sánti, grándi, buóni.*

Before a vowel: *bell', Sant', grand', buon;* pl. *bégli, Sánti, grándi, buóni.*

When used *after* a noun or in the predicate these adjectives have their full forms (*béllo, bélli, Sánto, Sánti, gránde, grándi, buóno, buóni*).

Ex.: *Un bel quádro,* a fine picture; *dùe béi létti,* two fine beds.
Un béllo scaffále, a fine bookcase; *quáttro bégli stiváli,* four fine boots.
Un bell' ándito, a fine hall; *mólti bégli orológi,* many fine clocks.
Una bélla stúfa, a fine stove; *parécchie bélle tènde,* several fine curtains.
Il palázzo è béllo, the palace is fine; *le sédie son bélle,* the chairs are beautiful.
San Piètro, Sánto Stéfano e Sant' Antònio, St. Peter, St. Stephen, and St. Anthony.
Un gran fuóco, a big fire; *grándi camini,* big fire-places.

Il grànde scaldìno, the big foot-warmer; *dièci gràndi spìlli*, ten big pins.

Un grànde sciàme, a great swarm; *il grànde zìpolo*, the large bung.

Un grand' armàdio, a big wardrobe; *vènti gràndi àlberi*, twenty big trees.

Úna grànde càmera, a large bedroom; *cìnque gràndi finèstre*, five big windows.

Il salòtto è mòlto grànde, the parlor is very large.

Un buon lùme, a good lamp; *buòni fiammìferi*, good matches.

Il buòno sgabèllo, the good stool; *nòve buòni scolàri*, nine good pupils.

Il buon òlio, the good oil; *parècchi buòni àghi*, several good needles.

Úna buòna cucìna, a good kitchen; *le buòne candèle*, the good candles.

Il bambìno è buòno, the child is good.

30. Any adjective of either gender or either number may be used as a noun.

Ex.: *I buòni*, the good; *la bèlla*, the beautiful woman.

COMPARISON.

31. All Italian adjectives form their comparative by prefixing *più* "more," and their superlative by prefixing the definite article to the comparative. When the superlative immediately follows the noun, this article is omitted.

Ex.: *Bèllo*, beautiful; *più bèllo*, more beautiful; *il più bèllo*, the most beautiful.

Lùngo, long; *più lùngo*, longer; *il più lùngo*, the longest.

La via più còrta, the shortest way.

a. The following adjectives have an irregular comparison in addition to the regular one: —

Àlto, high; *più àlto* or *superiòre*; *il più àlto* or *il superiòre*.

Bàsso, low; *più bàsso* or *inferiòre*; *il più bàsso* or *l'inferiòre*.

Buôno, good; *più buôno* or *migliôre;* * *il più buôno* or *il migliôre.*

Cattivo, bad; *più cattivo* or *peggiôre;* * *il più cattivo* or *il peggiôre.*

Grânde, big; *più grânde* or *maggiôre; il più grânde* or *il maggiôre.*

Piccolo, small; *più piccolo* or *minôre; il più piccolo* or *il minôre.*

"Higher" and "lower" are commonly rendered by *più âlto* and *più bâsso;* *superiôre* and *inferiôre* generally mean "superior" and "inferior." *Migliôre* and *peggiôre* are more used than *più buôno* and *più cattivo,* which have the same sense. "Larger" and "smaller" are generally *più grânde* and *più piccolo; maggiôre* and *minôre* usually signify "older" and "younger."

> Ex.: *Noi siâmo migliôri di lôro,* we are better than they.
>
> *Quésta sâla da prânzo è la più grânde,* this dining-room is the biggest.
>
> *Piêtro è il fratêllo minôre,* Peter is the youngest brother.

32. The adverb "less" is expressed by *méno,* "least" by *il méno.* "As . . . as," "so . . . as" are *tânto . . . quânto, tânto . . . côme, così . . . côme,* or simply *quânto.*

> Ex.: *Quélla stânza è la méno bellîna,* that room is the least pretty.
>
> *Pâolo non è tânto buôno côme Robêrto,* Paul isn't so good as Robert.
>
> *Giovânni è âlto quânto Filîppo,* John is as tall as Philip.

33. "Than" is *che.*

> Ex.: *L' albêrgo è più grânde che bêllo,* the hotel is bigger than it is beautiful.

But before a noun, a pronoun, or a numeral "than" is *di.* If, however, this "than" is preceded by a word meaning "rather" or its contrary, it is translated *che.*

---

* The *adverbs* "better" and "worse" are *mêglio* and *pêggio.*

Ex.: *Riccárdo è peggióre di Gugliélmo*, Richard is worse than
William.
Vói siéte più ricchi di nói, you are richer than we.
Méno di cínque, less than five.
Piuttósto la mórte che il disonóre, rather death than dishonor.

Before an inflected verb "than" is *che non* or *di quel
che*.

Ex.: *Abbáia più che non mórde*, he barks more than he bites.
Prométto méno di quel che do, I promise less than I give.

34. "The more ... the more," "the less ... the less"
are *più ... più, méno ... méno*. "More" and "less" after
a number are *di più, di méno*. In speaking of time,
"longer" after a negative is *più*.

Ex.: *Più stúdio, più impáro*, the more I study, the more I learn.
Trénta giórni di méno, thirty days less.
Non lo vediámo più, we see him no longer.

Il sóle è[1] un glóbo grandíssimo e sêmpre infocáto: ésso è[1]
gránde óltre un milióne di vólte più délla têrra; e díre[2] che
a' nôstri ôcchi apparísce[3] tánto più píccolo ! Ánche la lúna, che
splênde[4] duránte la nôtte, è[1] rotónda, ma è[1] mólto più píccola
délla têrra, e gíra[5] intórno a quésta[6] continovaménte. La lúna
non ha[1] lúce da sè, ma la ricéve[7] dal sóle. Êcco[8] perchè la lúna
óra la vediámo[9] e óra non la vediámo[9] più, óra ne vediámo[9]
mêzza, óra uno spícchio, óra un po' più, óra un po' méno, secóndo
che di éssa ci si presênta[10] úna párte maggióre o minóre illumi-
náta dal sóle. Le stélle sóno[1] tútti quéi[11] púnti luminósi che
vediámo[9] brilláre di[12] nôtte nel firmaménto. Non crediáte,[13] però,
che le stélle síano[1] píccole cóme nói le vediámo[9]: ci páiono[14]
così piccíne per la smisuráta distánza che córre[15] da lóro a nói;
ma le stélle sóno[1] grandíssime, e ce n'è di quélle[16] che sóno[1] in-

finitaménte più grándi del sóle. Gli è[1] che il sóle è[1] méno lontáno di ésse dálla têrra che nói abitiámo.[17]

[1] *È* = is; *sóno, stano* (subj.) = are; *ha* -- has. [2] To think. [3] It seems. [4] Shines. [5] Turns. [6] It. [7] *La ricéve* = receives it. [8] That is. [9] *Vedidmo* = we see; *la vedidmo* : we see it; *le vedidmo* = we see them; *ne vedidmo* = we see of it. [10] *Ci si presénta* = there presents itself to us. [11] Those. [12] At. [13] *Non credidte* — do not think. [14] *Ci pdiono* = they seem to us. [15] Intervenes. [16] *Ce n' è di quélle* = there are some. [17] Inhabit.

EXERCISE 6.

The moon is[1] in the middle of[2] the sky. The moon is[1] round; it-looks[3] perfectly round like a melon. And it-looks,[3] too, as big as a melon. The moon seems[4] little because it-is[1] far, far from us who are[5] on the earth. The moon renders[6] a great service to men : because when everything is[1] dark, it[7] illumines[8] with its beautiful light the earth which we-inhabit.[9] The stars are[10] larger than the moon, but to-look-at-them[11] they-seem[12] smaller, because they-are[10] so-much[13] further than the moon. The most beautiful,[14] the most intense[14] light comes[15] from the sun.

[1] *È.* [2] *A.* [3] *Par* or *pdre.* [4] *Si véde.* [5] *Sidmo.* [6] *Fa.* [7] *Éssa.* [8] *Rischidra.* [9] *Abitiámo.* [10] *Sóno.* [11] *A vedérle.* [12] *Pdiono.* [13] *Tánto.* [14] Both adjectives follow the noun. [15] *Viéne.*

AUGMENTATIVES AND DIMINUTIVES; NUMERALS.

AUGMENTATIVE AND DIMINUTIVE ENDINGS.

35. Instead of a word expressing size or quality the Italians often use a suffix. This suffix may be added to a noun, an adjective, or an adverb. When added to an adjective, and generally when added to a noun, it takes the gender of the word to which it is affixed: occasionally, however, a suffix with masculine termination is added to a feminine noun, which thereby becomes masculine. A word loses its final vowel before a suffix; but the preceding consonant, if it be *c* or *g*, must keep its former quality: as *Cárlo* + *ino* = *Carlíno*, *vóce* + *óne* = *vocióne*, *póco* + *ino* = *pochíno*, *adágio* + *ino* = *adagíno*.

a. The commonest ending is *-íssimo* (fem. *-íssima*), "very," which in general is added only to adjectives and adverbs. Adverbs in *-ménte* add the *-íssima* before the *-ménte* (see **85**). Any adjective may take it, and it is very often used in cases where it would be entirely superfluous in English.

> Ex.: *Lárgo*, wide; *larghíssimo*, very wide.
> *Béne*, well; *beníssimo*, very well.
> *Gránde*, big; *grandíssimo*, very big.
> *Fa un témpo bellíssimo*, it's beautiful weather.
> *Bellíssimaménte*, very beautifully.

b. The principal suffix denoting bigness is *-óne;* it is always masculine, but has a rare feminine form, *-óna.*

> Ex.: *Líbro*, book; *libróne*, big book.
> *Cása*, house; *casóne*, large house.
> *Bóccia*, decanter; *bocci óna*, big decanter.

c. The most important suffixes denoting smallness are *-íno,* *-cíno, -icíno, -iccíno, -étto, -éllo, -céllo, -icéllo, -aréllo, -eréllo, -ótto, -úccio, -úzzo, -uólo,* with their fem. *-ína,* etc. These endings, especially *-úccio,* are often used to express affection; some of them may be used to express pity or contempt. *Ótto* sometimes means "somewhat large" instead of "small."

> Ex.: *Sorélla*, sister; *sorellína*, little sister.
> *Béllo*, beautiful; *bellíno*, pretty.
> *Brútto*, ugly; *bruttíno*, rather ugly.
> *Piázza*, square; *piazzétta*, little square.
> *Giórgio*, George; *Giorgétto*, Georgie.

Campána, bell; *campanéllo,* little bell.
Áquila, eagle; *aquilótto,* eaglet.
Cása, house; *casótta,* rather large house.
Giovánni, John; *Giovannúccio,* dear little Johnny.
Pázzo, mad; *pazzarélla,* poor mad woman.
Póvero, poor; *poverini,* poor things!

d. The ending *-áccio* denotes worthlessness.

Ex.: *Róba,* stuff, goods; *robáccia,* trash.
Témpo, weather; *tempáccio,* nasty weather.
Alfrédo, Alfred; *Alfreddáccio,* naughty Alfred.

36. Of the endings added to nouns *-íno* is by far the most common; the only ones that are freely used to form new compounds are *-íno,* "little," *-óne,* "great," *-úccio,* "dear," and *-áccio,* "bad." In very many cases endings lose their character of independent suffixes, and become inseparable parts of certain words, whose meanings they often change: as *scála,* "stairway"; *scalíno,* "stair"; *scalétto,* "ladder." Some suffixes (as *-uólo*) are rarely used except in this way. Others (as *-cíno, -icíno, -éllo, -céllo, -icéllo, -aréllo, -créllo*) cannot be attached to any word at pleasure, their use being determined by precedent or euphony; those beginning with *c* are used only after *n.*

37. Sometimes several suffixes are added at once to the same word: as *ládro,* "thief"; *ladróne,* "terrible thief"; *ladroncéllo,* "terrible little thief."

NUMERALS.

38. The cardinal numerals are: —

1, *úno.*	5, *cínque.*	9, *nóve.*	13, *trédici.*
2, *dúe.*	6, *séi.*	10, *diéci.*	14, *quattórdici.*
3, *tre.*	7, *sétte.*	11, *úndici.*	15, *quíndici.*
4, *quáttro.*	8, *ótto.*	12, *dódici.*	16, *sédici.*

17, *diciasêtte.*	26, *ventisêi.*	50, *cinquânta.*	125, *cento venti-*
18, *diciôtto.*	27, *ventisêtte.*	60, *sessânta.*	*cinque.*
19, *diciannôve.*	28, *ventôtto* or	70, *settânta.*	200, *dugênto* or
20, *vênti.*	*vent' ôtto.*	80, *ottânta.*	*duecênto.*
21, *ventùno* or	29, *ventinôve.*	90, *novânta.*	250, *dugênto cin-*
vent' úno.	30, *trênta.*	100, *cênto.*	*quânta.*
22, *ventidúe.*	31, *trentùno* or	101, *centùno* or	300, *trecênto.*
23, *ventitrè.*	*trent' úno.*	*cent' úno.*	400, *quattrocênto.*
24, *ventiquâttro.*	32, *trentadúe.*	105, *centocinque.*	1000, *mílle.*
25, *venticinque.*	40, *quarânta.*	115, *centoquindici.*	2000, *dúe míla.*

Úno has a feminine *úna ;* when used adjectively *úno* has the same forms as the indefinite article. The plural of *mílle* is *míla.* "A million" is *un milióne* or *millióne*, of which the plural is *milióni* or *millióni.*

(1) No conjunction is used between the different parts of a number : as *dugênto quarânta,* "two hundred and forty." No indefinite article is used before *cênto* and *mílle :* as *cênto líbri,* "a hundred books."

(2) *Cênto, dugênto,* etc., when followed by another numeral of more than two syllables may lose the final syllable *-to :* as *scicênto cinquánta* or *scicencinquánta,* "six hundred and fifty."

(3) "Eleven hundred," "twelve hundred," etc., must be rendered *millecênto, mílle dugênto,* etc. : as *mílle ottocênto ottantasêtte,* 1887.

(4) "Both," "all three," etc., are *tútti* (fem. *tútte*) *e dúe, tútti* (fem. *tútte*) *e tre,* etc.

a. If the noun modified by *ventúno, trentúno,* etc., follows the numeral, it should be in the singular ; if it precedes, in the plural.

Ex.: *Sessantúna líra* or *líre sessantúna,* 61 francs.

b. In dates the definite article is prefixed to the number representing the year, if that number follows a preposition, or does not follow the name of a month.

Ex.: *Nel mille ottocènto ottantasètte*, in 1887.

c. "What time is it?" is *che óra è?* "It is six," etc., is *sóno le sèi*, etc., *óre* being understood. "One o'clock" is *il tócco*.

Ex.: *Sóno le dùe e mèzzo*, it's half-past two.
Sóno le tre e dièci, it's ten minutes past three.
Ci máncano vènti minùti álle quáttro, it's twenty minutes to four.
Sóno le cinque mèno un quárto, it's a quarter to five.

39. The ordinal numerals are : —

1st, *primo.*	12th, *duodècimo* or	20th, *ventèsimo.*
2d, *secóndo.*	*dècimo secóndo.*	21st, *ventèsimo primo* or
3d, *tèrzo.*	13th, *tredicèsimo* or	*ventunèsimo.*
4th, *quárto.*	*dècimo tèrzo.*	22d, *ventèsimo secóndo*
5th, *quìnto.*	14th, *quattordicèsimo* or	or *ventiduèsimo.*
6th, *sèsto.*	*dècimo quárto.*	30th, *trentèsimo.*
7th, *sèttimo.*	15th, *quindicèsimo* or	100th, *centèsimo.*
8th, *ottávo.*	*dècimo quìnto.*	101st, *centèsimo primo.*
9th, *nóno.*	16th, *dècimo sèsto.*	115th, *centoquindicèsimo.*
10th, *dècimo.*	17th, *dècimo sèttimo.*	200th, *dugentèsimo.*
11th, *undècimo* or	18th, *dècimo ottávo.*	1000th, *millèsimo.*
dècimo primo.	19th, *dècimo nóno.*	2000th, *duemilèsimo.*

All of them form their feminines and plurals like other adjectives in *o.*

Ex.: *Le settantèsime quìnte cóse*, the 75th things.

a. Ordinal numerals are used after the words "book," "chapter," and the names of rulers; but no article intervenes.

Ex.: *Cárlo secóndo*, Charles the Second; *Pio nóno*, Pius IX.
Libro tèrzo, Book the Third; *capìtolo quárto*, chapter four.

b. For the day of the month, except the first, a cardinal number is used.

Ex.: *Il dì cinque d' aprile* or *il cinque aprile*, the fifth of April.
Il primo di mággio, the first of May.

c. "A third," "a fourth," "a fifth," etc., are *un tèrzo, un quárto, un quinto*, etc. "Half" is *la metà;* the adjective "half" is
mèzzo.

40. "A couple" or "a pair" is *un páio.* "A dozen"
is *úna dozzína.* The expressions *úna decína, úna ventína,
úna trentína*, etc., *un centináio, un migliáio*, mean "about
ten," "about twenty," etc. "Once," "twice," etc., are
úna vólta, dúe vólte, etc.

> Ex.: *Un páio di scárpe*, a pair of shoes.
> *Úna cinquantína di persóne*, some fifty persons.
> *L' ho visto parécchie vólte*, I've seen it several times.

EXERCISE 7.

Con l' orológio si véde[1] che óre sóno.[2] Un giórno è[3] ventiquáttr' óre. Cèrte óre del giórno è[2] lúme, cèrte óre è[2] búio. Un
giórno è[3] ventiquáttr' óre, ma súlla móstra dell' orológio, délle óre
ce n' è[4] segnáte dódici, perchè le óre del giórno si cóntano[5] dall-
l' úna álle dódici, così : tócco, dúe, tre, quáttro, cínque, sèi, sètte,
òtto, nòve, dièci, úndici e dódici. Arriváti a dódici non si séguita[6] a díre trédici, quattórdici, e vía fíno a ventiquáttro ; ma si
ricomíncia[7] da cápo dal tócco e si arríva[8] fíno a dódici. Il cónto
tórna[9] lo stésso : infátti le óre del giórno son[11] ventiquáttro ; e
dódici e dódici, sommáti insiême, fórmano[10] ventiquáttro. Dódici
óre sóno[11] la metà del giórno. L' orológio ha[12] dódici óre ; e le
ha[13] segnáte gíro gíro álla móstra. L' óra è[3] sessánta minúti ; e
l' orológio ségna[14] ánche i minúti. Quélle righettíne tórno tórno
álla móstra, fra un' óra e un' áltra, sóno[11] i sessánta minúti che
fórmano[10] l' óra. La lancétta gránde ségna[14] i minúti. La lancétta piccína ségna[14] le óre. La lancétta gránde ógni óra fa[15] il
gíro di tútti e sessánta i minúti ; gíra[16] tútta la móstra. La lancétta píccola ógni óra ségna[14] un número, e a girár tútta la móstra
ci métte[17] dódici óre, perchè dódici son[11] le óre segnáte súlla mó-

stra. Óra sóno[2] le dódici; tútte e dúe le lancétte sóno[11] súlle dódici. Fra un' óra la lancétta gránde avrà[13] giráta tútta la móstra, e sarà[19] daccápo sul número 12, e la lancétta piccína sarà[19] sull' úno.

[1] *Si véde* = we see. [2] It is. [3] Is. [4] *Ce n' è* = there are. [5] *Si cóntano* = are counted. [6] *Non si séguita* = we don't go on. [7] *Si ricomíncia* = we begin over again. [8] *Si arriva* = we go. [9] Amounts to. [10] Make. [11] Are. [12] Has. [13] *Le ha* = it has them. [14] Marks. [15] Makes. [16] It goes around. [17] *Ci métte* = it takes. [18] Will have. [19] Will be.

EXERCISE 8.

A year is[1] 365 days. Every seven days is[1] a week. The days of the week are-called[2]: Sunday, Monday, Tuesday, Wednesday, Thursday, Friday, Saturday. Sunday[3] is[1] a[4] holiday; the other days we-work,[5] and therefore they-are-called[2] working-days. The year is-divided[6] into twelve months. The months are-called[2]: January, February, March, April, May, June, July, August, September, October, November, December. The month is[1] thirty or thirty-one days. When the month begins,[7] it-is-called[8] the first of the month; the second day is-called[8] the second of the month, the third, the third, and so-on[9] until the thirtieth or thirty-first. January, March, May, July, August, October, and[4] December have[10] thirty-one days. April, June, September, and[4] November have[10] thirty days. February is[1] the shortest month, because it-has[11] twenty-eight days only.[12] But every four years February has[11] twenty-nine days; and that[16] year is-called[13] leap-year. The year begins[7] from January; January is,[1] then,[14] the first month of the year. The year ends[15] with December; so[14] December is[1] the last month of the year.

[1] *È.* [2] *Si chiámano.* [3] Use def. article. [4] Omit. [5] *Si lavóra.* [6] *Si divíde.* [7] *Comíncia.* [8] *Si díce.* [9] *Così.* [10] *Hánno.* [11] *Ha.* [12] *Sóli.* [13] *Si chiáma.* [14] *Dúnque.* [15] *Finísce.* [16] *Quell'.*

DEMONSTRATIVE, INTERROGATIVE, RELA-
TIVE, AND POSSESSIVE PRONOUNS.

41. For the indefinite pronouns, see **86–91**.

42. (1) The demonstrative pronouns used adjectively
are *quésto*, "this," and *quéllo* or *cotésto*, "that." *Cotésto* is
used only of objects near the person addressed. *Quésto*
and *cotésto* are inflected like other adjectives ; but they
generally drop *o* before a vowel. *Quéllo* is inflected like
béllo (see **29**, *c*).

> Ex.: *Quest' uómo*, this man ; *quéste ragázze*, these girls.
> *Quel bambíno*, that infant ; *quéi fanciúlli*, those children.
> *Quell' amíco*, that friend ; *quégli spósi*, that couple.
> *Quéllo zío*, that uncle ; *quélle signóre*, those ladies.

Quésto and *quéllo* are also used substantively for "this,"
"that," "this one," "that one" : as *fáte quésto, non fáte
quéllo*, "do this, don't do that."

(2) "This man" is translated by *quésti*, "that man"
by *quégli, quéi*, or *cotésti* (rare) ; these words are invariable, refer only to persons, and are used only in the nominative singular. *Costúi* and *colúi* mean respectively the
same as *quésti* and *quégli*, but are not defective, having
a feminine singular *costéi, coléi*, and a plural (both genders
alike) *costóro, colóro*. *Costúi* is often used in a deprecia-
tive sense.

> Ex.: *Quésti è francése e quégli è tedésco*, this man is French and
> that one is German.
> *Chi è costúi*, who is this fellow?
> *Párlo di colúi*, I speak of that man.

(3) *Ciò*, "this," "that," is invariable, and represents a whole idea, not a single word: as *ciò è véro*, "that's so."

a. *Quéllo* and *quésto, quégli* and *quésti* mean also "the former," "the latter."

b. "He who" is *colúi che*, or simply *chi*. "The one who, whom, which," "that which," "what" is *quéllo che* or *quel che*.

Ex.: *Chi lavóra* or *colúi che lavóra*, he who works.
    Quel che dico io, the one I mean.
    A quel che sènto, from what I hear.

43. The interrogative "who," "whom," is *chi*. "What?" used substantively is *che, che côsa*, or *côsa*.* "What?" used adjectively is *che* or *quále*. "Which?" is *quále*. *Quále* has a plural *quáli; chi* and *che* are invariable. "How much?" is *quánto (-a)*, "how many?" is *quánti (-e)*.

Ex.: *Chi védo*, whom do I see?
    Di chi parláte, of whom do you speak?
    Che côsa dice, what does he say?
    Che or *quáli libri avéte compráto*, what books did you buy?
    Quále di quésti volúmi è il prímo, which of these volumes is
      the first?

a. The interrogative "whose" is *di chi*.

Ex.: *Di chi è quésto bigliétto*, whose card is this?

b. In exclamations "what a," "what," are rendered by *che* or *quále* without any article.

Ex.: *Che bel paése*, what a beautiful country!

44. The principal relative pronouns are *che, cúi, il quále:* they are all applied to both persons and things, and mean "who, "whom," "which," or "that." *Il quále* is inflected

---

* *Côsa* (as *côsa dice?*) is generally avoided in written Italian.

(*la quále, i quáli, le quáli*). *Che* and *cúi* are invariable: in general *che* is used only as subject and direct object, *cúi* only after prepositions or as indirect object.

> Ex.: *La lingua che si párla*, the language which we speak.
> *L' uómo del quále si trátta*, the man of whom we are speaking.
> *Le persóne a cúi* or *álle quáli párlo*, the persons to whom I speak.
> *Lo scrítto di cúi párlo*, the work I am speaking of.
> *Égli è colúi, cúi fu dáto*, he is the man to whom it was given.

(1) As subject or direct object *che* is preferred to *il quále*, unless clearness requires the latter.

(2) The relative "whose" is *il cúi* or *del quále*.

> Ex.: *Úna signóra, il cúi nóme è Lucía*, a lady whose name is Lucy.
> *Un uómo, le cúi fíglie conósco*, a man whose daughters I know.
> *L' autóre, del cúi libro si párla*, the author whose book we are speaking of.
> *Le chiése délle quáli si védono le cúpole*, the churches whose domes we see.

(3) The relative cannot be omitted in Italian.

> Ex.: *Le cáse che ho compráte*, the houses I have bought.

a. "Such . . . as" is *tále . . . quále;* in poetry *tále* has a plural *tái* instead of *táli*. "As much as" is *tánto quánto;* "as many as" is *tánti quánti*.

> Ex.: *Quále è il pádre tále è il fíglio*, as is the father, so is the son.

b. "He who" is *chi* or *colúi che* (see **42**, *b*).

> Ex.: *Chi ha la sanità è ricco*, he who has health is rich.

c. "Whoever" is *chiúnque;* "whatever" as a substantive is *tútto quel che* or *checchè*, as an adjective *quále che, qualúnque che, qualúnque, per quánto*. These words, excepting *tútto quel che*, all take the subjunctive. *Checchè* is now but little used.

Ex.: *Chiúnque sídte*, whoever you may be.
Checchè facciáte, fátelo bène, whatever you do, do it well.
Tútto quel che volète, whatever you wish.
Quáli che síano i vóstri motívi, whatever your motives may be.
Qualúnque síano i suói talènti, whatever his talents may be.
In qualúnque státo che io mi tróvi, in whatever condition I may find myself.
Per quánte ricchèzze ègli ábbia, whatever riches he may have.

45. The possessive pronouns are : —

My :	m.,	*il mio,*	f., *la mía,*	m. pl., *i miéi,*	f. pl., *le mie.*
Thy :		*il túo,*	*la túa,*	*i tuói,*	*le túe.*
His, her, its :		*il súo,*	*la súa,*	*i suói,*	*le súe.*
Our :		*il nóstro,*	*la nóstra,*	*i nóstri,*	*le nóstre.*
Your :		*il vóstro,*	*la vóstra,*	*i vóstri,*	*le vóstre.*
Their :		*il lóro,*	*la lóro,*	*i lóro,*	*le lóro.*

Lóro is invariable ; the others agree with the object possessed : as *il mío náso*, "my nose " ; *la súa bócca*, "his, her mouth" ; *i vóstri ócchi*, "your eyes" ; *le lóro lábbra*, "their lips."

When the possessive stands alone in the predicate, the article is omitted if the possessive is used adjectively.

Ex.: *Quésto cappèllo è mío*, this hat is *mine.*
Quésto cappèllo è il mío, this hat is mine (*i.e.*, the one that belongs to me).

a. The article is omitted before the possessive : (1) When a numeral, an adjective of quantity, or a demonstrative pronoun precedes it : as *quésto túo difètto*, "this fault of thine." (2) When the possessive forms part of a title : as *Vóstra Maestà*, "Your Majesty"; *Súa Altèzza*, "His Highness." (3) When the possessive modifies a noun used in the vocative (in this case the possessive generally follows its noun) : as *amíco mío*, "my friend !" (4) The article is generally omitted also when the possessive modifies a noun in the singular expressing relationship : as *nôstra mádre,* " our mother." But if the noun has a diminutive ending, or an adjective precedes the noun, the article is not omitted : as *il túo fratellíno,* " thy little brother " ; *la vôstra gentilíssima so- rélla,* " your kind sister." When the possessive *follows* the noun of relationship, the article is used before the noun : as *il cugíno vôstro,* " your cousin." (5) The article is omitted also in certain phrases, such as : *da párte mia,* " for me " ; *per amór mio,* " for my sake " ; *in cása nôstra,* " in our house " ; *a môdo súo,* " in his own way " ; *è côlpa vôstra,* " it's your fault."

b. The possessive, when not necessary for clearness, is usually replaced by a definite article.

Ex. : *Côme sta la mámma,* how is your mother?
Ha perdúto il giudízio, he has lost his senses.
Báttono i pièdi, they stamp their feet.

c. When the name of the thing possessed is direct object of a verb, the Italians often use instead of the possessive a conjunctive personal pronoun (see **47**) and a definite article. If the thing possessed be a part of the body or clothing, this construction is frequent, even when the name of the thing is not object of a verb.

Ex. : *Si stráppa i capélli,* he tears his hair (lit., he tears to himself the hairs).
Mi táglio il díto, I cut my finger (I cut to myself the finger).
Il cáne gli agguantò la gámba, the dog seized his leg (seized to him the leg).
Mi duôle il cápo, my head aches (to me aches the head).

d. When the possessor is not the subject of the sentence, " his," " her " are, for the sake of clearness, often rendered *di lúi, di léi.*

Ex. : *Égli non conôsce il di lèi cuôre,* he does not know her heart.

e. " A . . . of mine, of thine," etc., is *un mio, un túo,* etc.

Ex. : *Úna nôstra cugína,* a cousin of ours.

EXERCISE 9.

Quándo cádde[1] l' impêro, Siêna soffrì[2] méno délle áltre città toscáne dálle invasióni déi bárbari ; ma vénne[3] sótto la signoría déi Longobárdi, e pôi fu[4] úna délle città líbere di Carlomágno, néi cónti e baróni del quále, arricchíti dálle têrre e dái castêlli che diêde[5] lóro[6] l' imperatóre, i nôbili senési crédono[7] trováre l' orígine délla lóro nobiltà. Quésti ládri forestiêri, i cúi nídi néi dintórni di Firênze i cittadíni di quésto comúne cercávano[8] di distrúggere, abbandonárono[9] volontariaménte i lóro castêlli nel territôrio senése, ed entrárono[10] nélla città, che da éssi e dái véscovi veníva[4] abbellíta di grándi palázzi e governáta con úna máno di fêrro, finchè[11] i comúni non[11] si levárono[12] e non[11] fécero[13] prevalére il lóro diritto a participáre nélla côsa púbblica.

[1] Fell. [2] Suffered. [3] It came. [4] Was. [5] Gave. [6] To them. [7] Think, believe. [8] Were trying. [9] Abandoned. [10] Entered. [11] *Finchè non =* until. [12] *Si levárono =* arose. [13] Made.

EXERCISE 10.

Charles V made[1] of Siena a fief for his son Philip II, who ceded-it[2] to Cosimo I, and the latter built-there[3] the fort which the Spaniards had-tried-to[4] construct. The city remained[5] under the rule of the good dukes of Lorraine, until Napoleon made-it[6] capital of the department of the Ombrone. After the fall of the emperor, it-returned[7] under the dominion of the dukes. In[8] 1860 it-was[9] the first Tuscan city that voted[10] the union of Italy under Victor Emmanuel II, the only honest king of whom history speaks.[11]

[1] *Fêce.* [2] *La cedétte.* [3] *Vi fabbricò.* [4] *Avévano volúto.* [5] *Restò.* [6] *La fêce.* [7] *Ritornò.* [8] See **38,** *b.* [9] *Fu.* [10] *Votásse.* [11] *Párli,* which should precede its subject.

PERSONAL PRONOUNS.

46. Personal pronouns are divided into two classes, conjunctive and disjunctive : the conjunctive forms are those used as direct object of a verb, and as indirect object without a preposition ; the disjunctive forms are those used as subject of a verb, and as object of a preposition.

CONJUNCTIVE FORMS.

47. These forms are called conjunctive because they cannot be separated from the verb, which they sometimes follow but oftener precede, as will be explained in **48.**

They exist only in the objective case, being used either as direct object of a verb or as indirect object without a preposition. The forms are these : —

Mi, me, to me.	*Ti*, thee, to thee.
Ci, us, to us.	*Vi*, you, to you.

Si (reflexive), himself, to himself; herself, to herself.
Si (reflexive), themselves, to themselves.

Lo, him; *gli*, to him.	*La*, her; *le*, to her.
Li, them (masc.); *loro*, to them.	*Le*, them (fem.); *loro*, to them.

There being no neuter form of the personal pronoun in Italian, " it " must be rendered by a masculine or feminine form, according to the gender of the noun it represents. " It " representing not a word, but a whole clause, is *lo*.

Ex. : *Mi conósce*, he knows me ; *ti do i libri*, I give thee the books.
Ci vedéte, you see us ; *vi dico tútto*, I tell you everything.
Si véste, he dresses himself ; *si divértono*, they amuse themselves.
Vedéte quell' álbero ? — *Lo védo.* — " Do you see that tree ? " " I see it."
Vi piáce la Spágna ? — *Non la conósco.* — " Does Spain suit you ? " " I'm not acquainted with it."

Cóme potéva sapére se io veniva o no? — Lo ha indovináto. —
"How could he tell whether I was coming or not?" "He
guessed it."

(1) It will be seen that the third person (not reflexive)
has different forms for the direct and the indirect object.

Ex.: *Lo trováti,* I found him; *gli fici un regálo,* I made him a
present.
La láscia, he leaves her; *le scríve,* he writes to her.
Li cercáte, you seek them (masc.); *le salutáte,* you greet them
(fem.); *mandiámo lóro mille salúti,* we send them (masc.
or fem.) a thousand greetings.

(2) The reflexive pronouns of the first and second persons are: *mi, ci; ti, vi.* All reflexive pronouns are used
also as reciprocal pronouns.

Ex.: *Mi diféndo,* I defend myself; *vi lauáte,* you wash yourselves.
Si ódiano, they hate each other; *ci amiámo,* we love one
another.

(3) Another conjunctive pronoun is *ne,** "of it," "of
them"; it corresponds also to "any," "some" when these
words mean "any, some of it, of them." It is often used
pleonastically in Italian.

Ex.: *Ne párla,* he speaks of it; *ne ho,* I have some.
Non ne abbiámo, we haven't any; *ne voléte,* do you want any?
Tu ne approfítti di quésta libertà, you make good use of this
liberty.

a. Ci, "us," and *vi,* "you," must not be confounded with the
adverbs *ci, vi* meaning "here," "there," "to it," "to them," etc.†
These adverbs (see **84**) are very common in Italian, and are
often used pleonastically. There is also an adverb *ne** meaning
"thence," "from it," "from them."

---

* Cf. French *en.*   † Cf. French *y.*

Ex.: *Ci vádo*, I go there; *è tróppo básso per arrivárci*, he's too short to reach up to it.

A quéste cóse non ci pénso (*pensáre a* = to think of), I don't think of these things.

Ne tornerà dománi, he will return from there to-morrow.

48. The conjunctive pronouns, except *lóro*, immediately precede the verb : as *mi vedéte*, "you see me"; *non lo capísco*, "I don't understand him."

But when the verb is an infinitive,* a participle, or a positive imperative,† the pronoun follows the verb, and is written as one word with it : as *per vedérlo*, "to see him "; *di avérlo veduto*, "to have seen him "; *vedéndoci*, "seeing us "; *avéndoci veduto*, "having seen us "; *vedútoti*, "having seen thee "; *vedételi*, "see them." The addition of the pronoun does not change the place of the accent.

Lóro always follows the verb, but is never united to it : as *égli dà lóro del víno*, "he gives them some wine"; *parláte lóro*, "speak to them."

a. When a conjunctive pronoun is object of an infinitive immediately dependent on another verb, it may either be attached to the infinitive or be placed as if governed by the other verb.

Ex.: *Pòsso vedérti* or *ti pòsso vedére*, I can see thee.

b. When a conjunctive pronoun is joined to an infinitive, that infinitive drops its final *e* ; if it ends in *-rre*, it drops *-re*.

Ex.: *Fárlo* (*fáre*), to do it ; *condúrvi* (*condúrre*), to conduct you.

---

* Not the infinitive used (with a negative) as imperative (see **72**) : as *non lo fáre*, " do not do it."

† Not the subjunctive (see **77,** *a*) nor the negative imperative. Ex.: *Si régoli* (third pers. sing. pres. subj.), "let him moderate himself "; *non li guardáte*, " do not look at them."

c. The final vowel of *mi, ti, si, lo, la* is often elided (that of *lo, la* nearly always) before a verb beginning with a vowel.

Ex.: *T' amo,* I love thee; *l' ho visto,* I've seen him.

d. All conjunctive pronouns except *gli* and *glie* (see **50**) double their initial consonant when added to any form of a verb that ends in an accented vowel.

Ex.: *Dámmi* (imper. *da'* from *dáre*), give me.
Dillo (imper. *di* from *dire*), say it.
Parlerólle (antique, for *le parlerò*), I shall speak to her.

e. The adverbs *ne, ci,* and *vi* occupy the same positions as the conjunctive pronouns (see **47**, *a*).

f. Pronouns are joined to the interjection *ecco,* "see here," just as they are joined to the imperative of a verb.

Ex.: *Éccomi,* here I am; *eccole,* here they are.
Éccotelo prónto, here it is ready for thee.

49. When two conjunctive pronouns come together, the indirect object precedes the direct: as *mi vi presénta,* "he introduces you to me"; *non vuol presentárvimi,* "he will not introduce me to you"; *gli si presentò un uómo,* "a man presented himself to him."

Lóro, however, always comes last: as *presentátela lóro,* "introduce her to them."

Ne follows all forms except *lóro:* as *me ne dà,* "he gives me some"; *dátene lóro,* "give them some."

a. The adverbs *ne, ci,* and *vi* follow the pronouns of the first and second persons, but precede those of the third: *te ne cáccia,* "he drives you away from it"; *mi vi troverái,* "you will find me there"; *ce la mánda,* "he sends it here"; *ve lo trovái,* "I found him there." *Si,* however, always precedes *ne.*

50. *Mi, ti, ci, vi, si* change their *i* to *e* before *lo, la, gli, li, le, ne,* and are often united with them : as *me lo* (or *mélo*) *dice,* "he tells me it"; *ve ne* (or *véne*) *domándo,* "I ask you for some"; *mandátecelo,* "send it to us." *Gli* and *le* ("to her") become *glie* before *lo, la, li, le, ne,* and unite with them : as *gliéli mándo,* "I send them to him, to her"; *vôglio dárglielo,* "I wish to give it to him, to her."

DISJUNCTIVE FORMS.

51. These forms are so called because they do not necessarily stand next to the verb.

Disjunctive pronouns have two cases, nominative and objective. The objective case is used only after prepositions (for exceptions, see **51,** *a*).

The disjunctive forms are these : —

Io, I; *me,* me.	*Tu,* thou; *te,* thee.
Nôi, we; *nôi,* us.	*Vôi,* you; *vôi,* you.

{ *Égli, lùi, ésso,* he; *lùi, ésso,* him.
{ *Élla, léi, éssa,* she; *léi, éssa,* her.

{ *Éssi, lôro* (*églino*), they (masc.); *lôro, éssi,* them (masc.).
{ *Ésse, lôro* (*élleno*), they (fem.); *lôro, ésse,* them (fem.).

"It" must be rendered by a masculine or feminine form, according to the gender of the noun it represents. "It" as subject of an impersonal verb is regularly not expressed (see, however, **51,** *h*).

> Ex.: *La càsa è grandìssima, e intôrno ad éssa c' è un giardìno,* the house is very large, and around it there is a garden.
> *Non è véro,* it isn't true; *piôve,* it rains.

(1) The various pronouns of the third person are used as follows. In speaking of things the different forms of *ésso* are the ones commonly employed. In speaking of

persons *égli* (or *ésso*), *élla* (or *éssa*), pl. *éssi, ésse* are used for the nominative in written Italian, but in the spoken language they are replaced by *lúi, léi, lóro;* for the objective *lúi, léi, lóro* are used both in conversation and in writing. *Églino* and *élleno* are antique forms.

> Ex.: *Quéste cóse sóno vére anch' ésse*, these things are true too.
> *Élla párla con lóro*, she speaks with them.
> *Léi è gióvane ma lúi è vécchio*, she is young, but he is old.
> *Vénnero da nói anch' éssi*, they came to us too.

(2) As the Italian verb denotes by its endings the person and number of its subject, the personal pronouns of the nominative case are generally omitted. When expressed (for clearness, emphasis, or euphony), they may precede or follow the verb; but the subject of an interrogative verb must come after it, as in English.

> Ex.: *Parliámo di lúi*, we speak of him.
> *Non capíscono*, they don't understand.
> *S' io fóssi ricco cóme è égli*, if I were rich as he is.
> *Siéte sólo* or *siéte vói sólo*, are you alone?

(3) The disjunctive reflexive pronoun is *sè*, which is masculine and feminine, singular and plural.

> Ex.: *Lo fécero da sè*, they did it by themselves.

a. The objective case must be used: (1) In exclamations without a verb, unless the pronoun be of the second person: as *beáto lúi*, "happy he!"; *beáto tu*, "happy thou!" (2) After *cóme, quánto*, and *che* (= "as" or "than"), if the pronoun be of the third person: as *sóno vécchio quánto lóro*, "I am as old as they"; *tánto i genitóri che lúi*, "his parents as well as he." (3) When the pronoun stands in the predicate after the verb *éssere*: as *credéndo ch' io fóssi te*, "thinking I was you." But "it is I," etc., are *sóno io, sèi tu, è lúi, è léi, siámo nói, siéte vói, sóno lóro*.

b. (1) Clearness or emphasis occasionally requires the disjunctive pronoun instead of the conjunctive ; in this case the conjunctive form is often inserted also.

Ex.: *Párlo a vói signóre*, I speak to *you*, sir.
Mi piáce ánche a me, it pleases me too.

(2) The disjunctive form must always be used when the verb has two direct or two indirect objects.

Ex.: *Védo lúi e léi*, I see him and her.
Lo do a mío pádre e a te, I give it to my father and to thee.

c. In speaking of a company, a class, or a people *nói áltri, vói áltri* (which are also written as one word) are used for *nói, vói*.

Ex.: *Nói áltri italiáni*, we Italians.
Vói áltri pittóri, you painters.

d. "With me," "with thee," "with himself, herself, themselves " are *méco, téco, séco*.

e. "Myself," "thyself," etc., used for emphasis with a pronoun or noun, are rendered by the adjective *stésso*.

Ex.: *Nói stéssi la vedémmo*, we saw her ourselves.

f. "One another," "each other " is *l' un l' áltro*.

Ex.: *Ci amiámo l' un l'áltro*, we love one another.

g. In Florence *élla* is often shortened into *la*, which is used of both persons and things.

Ex.: *La non viéne*, she doesn't come.
Páre che la si póssa tenér in máno, it looks as if it might be held in the hand.

h. In impersonal phrases like "it is " the subject, "it," is occasionally expressed in Italian ; it is then translated *égli*, which in the spoken language is shortened into *gli*.

Ex.: *Gli è che*, it is because.

52. (1) The usual form of address in Italy is *Élla* * (or *élla*), objective *Léi* (or *léi*) ; in conversation *Ella* is replaced by *Léi* (or *léi*). This word really means " it," and takes the verb in the third person ; but an adjective or past participle modifying it agrees in gender with the person it represents. The plural of *Élla* is *Lóro* (or *lóro*), which takes the verb in the third person plural.

> Ex.: *Léi* or *Élla è tedésco, signóre,* you are German, sir.
> *Signorina Néri, Léi* (or *Élla*) *fu lasciáta sóla,* Miss Neri, you were left alone.
> *Sóno liéto che La stia béne* (see **51**, *g*), I'm glad you are well.
> *E Lóro, dóve vánno,* and you, where are you going?
> *Lóro érano già partiti,* you were already gone.
> *Signorine, lóro sóno mólto studióse,* young ladies, you are very studious.

Like other personal pronouns, *Élla* and *Lóro* are very often omitted in the nominative.

> *Léi è tróppo gentile* or *è tróppo gentile,* you are too kind.
> *Cóme stánno,* how do you (pl.) do?

The conjunctive forms of *Élla* are *La, Le* (or *la, le*), those of *Lóro* are *Li, Le, Lóro* (or *li, le, lóro*) ; they occupy the same positions and undergo the same modifications as the corresponding pronouns of the third person (see **48, 49, 50**). The reflexive pronoun of *Élla* and *Lóro* is *si*.

> Ex.: *Le prométto di visitárla,* I promise (you) to visit you.
> *Gliélo do,* I give it to you.
> *La prégo d' accomodársi,* I beg you to seat yourself.
> *Vidi Léi e il bábbo,* I saw you and your father (see **51**, *b*, 2).
> *Dico lóro,* I tell you (pl.).

---

* Standing for *Vóstra Signoría,* "your lordship" or "ladyship," or some other title of the feminine gender.

Le cercdva, I was looking for you (fem. pl.).
Si divèrtono, signorini, are you enjoying yourselves, young gentlemen?

The possessive of *Élla* is *Súo* (see 45).

Ex.: *La Súa gradíta lèttera,* your welcome letter.

(2) *Vói* is the form of address oftenest found in books; it is used sometimes in conversation also, but only toward inferiors or toward equals with whom one is on familiar terms.* It is employed for both plural and singular (like English "you"), although its verb is always plural; an adjective or participle modifying it agrees in gender and number with the person or persons it represents.

Ex.: *Vói qui, Piètro,* You here, Peter?
Vói siète álti tútti e dúe, you are tall, both of you.

(3) In speaking to an intimate friend, a near relative, a child, or an animal the only form of address is *tu.* *Tu* is used also, like English "thou," in poetry and poetic prose. The plural of *tu* is *vói.*

Ex.: *Ti chiámo Enrico,* I call you Henry.
Dóve sèi tu, where art thou?
Vóglio vedérvi, figliuóli mièi, my children, I wish to see you.

EXERCISE II.

Tant' è[1]! dicéva[2] tra sè un giórno Niccolíno; vóglio[3] vedére se quégli uccellíni son[4] náti. Li guárdo[5] solaménte e riscéndo[6] súbito. — E Niccolíno s' arrámpica[7] su per quell' álbero, tentándo[8] d' arriváre al nído per levársi quélla curiosità. Ma sul più bèllo,[9] sènte[10] la vóce del bábbo il quále èra[11] lì prèsso nélla viòttola;

---

* Though advocated by some of the best writers and. speakers of Italian, the use of *vói* instead of *Lèi* and *Lóro* has not become general. In Southern Italy, however, *vói* is the form popularly used.

vuôle[12] scénder lèsto per non fársi côgliere in fállo, ma nélla fúria si smarrísce,[17] gli mánca[14] il sostégno, precípita[15] a têrra, e cadêndo[16] si fa mále a[17] un piêde. Il dolóre lo fa[18] strilláre ; álle grída córrono[19] il bábbo e la mámma che lo raccôlgono[20] esclamándo[21] : — Te l' abbiámo[22] détto le cênto vôlte che a' nídi non ti dovévi[23] voltár nemméno : êcco quel che succêde[24] ai curiósi e a' disubbidiênti. — E sôrte per lúi che lo sentírono,[25] perchè così potérono[26] prónti bagnárgli il piêde coll' ácqua frédda, e dópo avérgliclo tenúto in quell' ácqua parécchio têmpo, potéron[26] fasciárglielo strétto ; in quésto môdo e dópo quálche giórno di ripôso assolúto, Niccolíno potè[27] ricominciáre a fáre quálche pásso per cása.

[1] I don't care. [2] Said. [3] I want. [4] Are. [5] I will look at. [6] Will come down again. [7] Climbs. [8] Trying. [9] *Sul più béllo* = at the critical moment. [10] He hears. [11] Was. [12] He tries. [13] He gets confused. [14] Fails. [15] He tumbles. [16] Falling. [17] *Fa mâle a* = he injures. [18] Makes. [19] Run. [20] Pick up. [21] Exclaiming. [22] We have. [23] *Non dovévi* = you mustn't. [24] Happens. [25] They heard. [26] They could. [27] Was able.

EXERCISE 12.

[In this exercise CARLINO and GORO use *vói;* ARMANDO uses *vói* before GORO enters, *Lêi* afterwards.]

Carlíno. Sir, we are[1] alone.

Armándo. So it seems[2] (*looking[3] around*).

Carlíno. I repeat[4] to you that we are[1] alone (*louder*).

Armándo. But I tell[5] you that I admit-it.[6]

Carlíno. It is[7] time to-raise[8] the mask —

Armándo. (Oh-my[9]! this-fellow[10] has[11] recognized me.)

Carlíno. And to[15] speak plainly.

Armándo. That is[7] what I wanted[12] to[15] do, but they interrupted[13] me all-the-time.[14]

Carlíno. Do[15] you see[16] that grove over-there?

Armándo. I see[17] it.

Carlíno. There nobody will-interrupt[18] you.

Armándo. Must[19] I go there to speak (*surprised*)?

Carlíno. We shall-go[20] together. .

Enter[15] GORO *with two guns.*

Carlíno. (*Taking*[21] *one of-them*) Take[22] the other.
Armándo. Thanks, I am[23] not[24] a[25] hunter.
Góro. Take[22] it, or-else[26] — (*brandishing*[27] *a thick club*).
Armándo. Willingly — to[28] satisfy you — excuse-me,[29] is[7] it loaded?
Carlíno. To-be-brief,[30] you hate[31] me; you must[32] hate me. I hate[33] you. So[47] over-there in that grove — at eighty paces from-each-other[34] — bang![35] Either you kill[36] me or I kill[37] you.
Armándo. But I have[38] n't[24] these sinister intentions, which-are[15] contrary to my principles.
Carlíno. In that[50] case you will-permit[39] this-man-to-amuse-himself-by-shaking[40] the dust from your[41] black coat with that club.
Armándo. No, indeed; what-are-you-thinking-of[42]? It would-be[43] too much-trouble[44]! (*Góro brandishes*[45] *the club*) Be-easy[46] with the club.
Carlíno. No? Then[47] Carolína must[48] be mine.
Armándo. You're-welcome-to-her.[49]
Carlíno. In that[50] case we are friends; but be-off[51] from[52] here, do-you-understand[53]?
Armándo. (What a[54] nice way they have[55] in this country!)

[1] *Siámo.* [2] *Pàre.* [3] *Guardándo.* [4] *Ripéto.* [5] *Díco.* [6] *Ne convéngo.* [7] *È.* [8] To (*di*) raise to one's self.... [9] *Ahi.* [10] See **42**, 2. [11] *Ha.* [12] *Volévo.* [13] *Hánno interrótto.* [14] Always. [15] Omit. [16] *Vedéte.* [17] *Védo.* [18] *Interromperà.* [19] *Dévo.* [20] *Andrémo.* [21] *Prendéndo.* [22] *Prendéte.* [23] *Sóno.* [24] *Non,* "not," must precede the verb. [25] See **16**, *a.* [26] *Altriménti.* [27] *Agitándo.* [28] *Per.* [29] *Scúsi.* [30] *Alle córte.* [31] *Odiáte.* [32] *Dovéte.* [33] *Odio.* [34] The one from the other. [35] *Brun.* [36] *Ammazzáte.* [37] *Ammázzo.* [38] *Ho.* [39] *Permetteréte.* [40] That this man amuses (*divérta*) himself to shake. [41] See **45**, *c.* [42] Seems-it (*páre*) to you? [43] *Sarèbbe.* [44] *Incómodo.* [45] *Agita.* [46] *Stia buóno.* [47] *Dúnque.* [48] *Déve.* [49] Take (*pigli,* subj.) her then (*púre*) for-yourself. [50] *Tal.* [51] *Vïa.* [52] *Di.* [53] *Intendéste.* [54] **43**, *b.* [55] *Hánno.*

AUXILIARY VERBS.

53. The irregular verbs *éssere*, "to be," and *avére*, "to have," are the ones most used as auxiliaries in Italian. They are conjugated as follows : —

a. **Infinitives :** *éssere,* to be; *éssere státo,* to have been.
Participles : *essêndo,* being; *essêndo státo,* having been; *státo,* been.

Indicative.

PRESENT.	IMPERFECT.	PRETERITE.	FUTURE.
Sóno,	*Èra,*	*Fúi,*	*Saró,*
sêi,	*êri,*	*fósti,*	*saráï,*
è,	*êra,*	*fu,*	*sará,*
siámo,	*eravámo.*	● *fúmmo.*	*sarémo,*
siête,	*eraváte.*	*fóste,*	*saréte,*
sóno.	*êrano.*	*fúrono.*	*saránno.*

PERFECT.	PLUPERFECT.	PRETERITE PERFECT.	FUTURE PERFECT.
Sóno státo (státa),	*Èra státo (státa),*	*Fúi státo (státa),*	*Saró státo (státa),*
etc.	etc.	etc.	etc.
siámo státi (státe),	*eravámo státi (státe),*	*fúmmo státi (státe),*	*sarémo státi (státe),*
etc.	etc.	etc.	etc.

Imperative.	Subjunctive.		Conditional.
	PRESENT.	IMPERFECT.	
	Sia,	*Fóssi,*	*Sarêi,*
Sii or *sia.*	*sia,*	*fóssi,*	*sarésti,*
	sia,	*fósse,*	*sarêbbe.*
	siámo,	*fóssimo,*	*sarémmo,*
siáte.	*siáte,*	*fóste,*	*saréste,*
●	*siano* or *sieno.*	*fóssero.*	*sarêbbero.*

	PERFECT.	PLUPERFECT.	PERFECT.
	Sia státo (státa),	*Fóssi státo (státa),*	*Sarêi státo (státa),*
	etc.	etc.	etc.

b. **Infinitives**: *avére*, to have; *avére avúto*, to have had.
Participles: *avéndo*, having; *avéndo avúto*, having had; *avúto*, had.

Indicative.

PRESENT.	IMPERFECT.	PRETERITE.	FUTURE.
Hò,	*Avéva,*	*Êbbi,*	*Avrò,*
hái,	*avévi,*	*avésti,*	*avrái,*
ha,	*avéva,*	*êbbe,*	*avrà,*
abbiámo,	*avevámo,*	*avémmo.*	*avrémo,*
avéte,	*aveváte,*	*avéste,*	*avréte,*
hánno.	*avévano.*	*êbbero.*	*avránno.*

PERFECT.	PLUPERFECT.	PRETERITE PERFECT.	FUTURE PERFECT.
Ho avúto,	*Avéva avúto,*	*Êbbi avúto,*	*Avrò avúto,*
etc.	etc.	etc.	etc.

Imperative.	Subjunctive.		Conditional.
	PRESENT.	IMPERFECT.	
	Abbia,	*Avéssi,*	*Avréi,*
Abbi,	*ábbi* or *ábbia,*	*avéssi,*	*avrésti,*
	ábbia,	*avésse,*	*avrébbe,*
	abbiámo,	*avéssimo,*	*avrémmo,*
abbiáte.	*abbiáte.*	*avéste,*	*avréste,*
	ábbiano.	*avéssero.*	*avrébbero.*

	PERFECT.	PLUPERFECT.	PERFECT.
	Abbia avúto,	*Avéssi avúto,*	*Avréi avúto,*
	etc.	etc.	etc.

54. (1) The auxiliary of the passive is *éssere*, "to be."

Ex.: *Sóno amáto*, I am loved.

(2) The future ("shall," "will") and the conditional ("should," "would") are formed in Italian without any auxiliary.

Ex.: *Io andrò ed égli verrà*, I shall go, and he will come.
Vorréi vedérlo, I should like to see him.

(3) The auxiliary of the perfect, pluperfect, and future perfect tenses is *avére*, "to have," if the verb be active and transitive. If the verb be intransitive, the auxiliary is nearly always *éssere*. If the verb be passive, reflexive, or reciprocal, the auxiliary is always *éssere*.

> Ex.: *Ho parláto*, I have spoken.
> *Avévano fátto quéste cóse*, they had done these things.
> *Saró venúto*, I shall have come; *è nevicáto*, it has snowed.
> *Mi sóno fátto mále*, I have hurt myself.
> *Le dónne si érano sbagliáte*, the women had made a mistake.

a. A past participle used with the auxiliary *éssere* must agree with the subject in gender and number.

> Ex.: *La ragázza è tornáta*, the girl has returned.
> *Le dónne si sóno disputáte*, the women have disputed.
> *La sorélla si è fátta mále*, our sister has hurt herself.

b. A past participle used with *avere* may or may not agree with its direct object, according to the choice of the writer.

> Ex.: *La bírra che avéva bevúto* or *bevúta*, the beer I had drunk.
> *Ho vedúto* or *vedúte mólte cóse*, I have seen many things.

c. The English auxiliary "do" is never expressed in Italian.

> Ex.: *Non viéne*, he does not come.

d. (1) The English periphrastic form ("am," "was," etc., followed by the present participle), denoting duration, is expressed in Italian either by the simple verb or by the proper tense of *stáre*, "to be" (see **92**, 4), followed by the present participle. But the periphrastic form denoting mere futurity must be rendered by the simple present or future.[*]

---

[*] If, however, this form be past in English, only through being dependent on a main verb in a past tense, it must be rendered by the conditional: as *disse che verrébbe*, "he said he was coming."

Ex.: *Io camminàva*, I was walking.
  Sta lavoràndo, he is working.
  Leggévano or *stàvano leggèndo*, they were reading.
  Dice che viène or *verrà*, he says he is coming.

(2) "To be," expressing a state or condition, is often rendered by *stàre*, instead of *èssere*. *Stàre per* or *èssere per* (followed by the infinitive) means "to be on the point of."

Ex.: *Còme sta ? — Sto bène, e Lèi ? —* "How are you?" "I'm well, and you?"
  Stàva per uscìre, I was just going out.

e. A verb with the auxiliary "used to" (or "would" = "used to") is translated either by the simple imperfect or by the infinitive with *solère*, "to be accustomed" (see **92**, 14).

Ex.: *Vi andàva* or *solèva andàre ógni séra*, he used to go there every evening.

f. *Venìre*, "to come" (see **92**, 154), and *rimanére*, "to remain" (see **92**, 16), are sometimes used as auxiliaries in the simple tenses of the passive, instead of *èssere*.

Ex.: *Il làdro vènne arrestàto*, the thief was arrested.
  Rimàsi sorpréso, I was surprised.

g. The third person of the passive is very often replaced by the reflexive construction with *si*. This construction is generally used also to render the English "they," "people," "we," in an indefinite sense, followed by a verb ; and is often equivalent even to a definite "we." It is employed even with a neuter verb.

Ex.: *Quésto libro si lègge*, this book is read.
  Quèlle còse si facèvano, those things were done.
  Si raccónta, it is related.
  La spàda che mi si diède, the sword that was given me.
  Si va spésso in campàgna, people often go into the country.
  Si vèdono moltissime còse, we see very many things.
  Se ne pàrla, people talk about it.

h. "To have a thing done" is *far fáre úna cósa* (see **92**, 2).

Ex.: *Il re lo féce ammazzáre*, the king had him killed.

55. Following is a synopsis of the compound tenses of an active transitive verb. In the paradigms given henceforth these tenses will be omitted. The use of the tenses is explained **69–77**.

Infinitive PERFECT:	*Avére trováto*, to have found.
Participle PERFECT:	*Avéndo trováto*, having found.
Indicative PERFECT:	*Ho trováto*, I have found.
PLUPERFECT:	*Avéva trováto*, I had found.
PRETERITE PERFECT:	*Ébbi trováto*, I had found.
FUTURE PERFECT:	*Avrò trováto*, I shall have found.
Conditional PERFECT:	*Avréi trováto*, I should have found.
Subjunctive PERFECT:	*Abbia trováto*, I have found.
PLUPERFECT:	*Avéssi trováto*, I had found.

56. Following are synopses of the compound tenses of neuter, reflexive, and passive verbs. In the paradigms given henceforth these forms will be omitted.

a. Following is a synopsis of the compound tenses of the neuter verb *veníre*, "to come" : —

Infinitive PERFECT:	*Éssere venúto*, to have come.
Participle PERFECT:	*Esséndo venúto*, having come.
Indicative PERFECT:	*Sóno venúto*, I have come.
PLUPERFECT:	*Éra venúto*, I had come.
PRETERITE PERFECT:	*Fúi venúto*, I had come.
FUTURE PERFECT:	*Sarò venúto*, I shall have come.
Conditional PERFECT:	*Saréi venúto*, I should have come.
Subjunctive PERFECT:	*Sia venúto*, I have come.
PLUPERFECT:	*Fóssi venúto*, I had come.

b. Following is a synopsis of the compound tenses of the reflexive verbs *alzársi* ("to raise one's self"), "to get up," and *andársene*, "to go away" : —

(1) *Alzársi.*

Infinitive PERFECT :   *Êssersi alzáto,* to have got up.
Participle PERFECT :   *Esséndosi alzáto,* having got up.
Indicative PERFECT :   *Mi sóno alzáto,* I have got up.
     PLUPERFECT :   *Mi éra alzáto,* I had got up.
     PRETERITE PERFECT : *Mi fúi alzáto,* I had got up.
     FUTURE PERFECT :   *Mi saró alzáto,* I shall have got up.
Conditional PERFECT :   *Mi saréi alzáto,* I should have got up.
Subjunctive PERFECT :   *Mi sia alzáto,* I have got up.
     PLUPERFECT :   *Mi fóssi alzáto,* I had got up.

(2) *Andársene.* *

Infinitive PERFECT :   *Êssersene andáto,* to have gone away.
Participle PERFECT :   *Esséndosene andáto,* having gone away.
Indicative PERFECT :   *Me ne sóno andáto,* I have gone away.
     PLUPERFECT :   *Me ne éra andáto,* I had gone away.
     PRETERITE PERFECT : *Me ne fúi andáto,* I had gone away.
     FUTURE PERFECT :   *Me ne saró andáto,* I shall have gone away.
Conditional PERFECT :   *Me ne saréi andáto,* I should have gone away.
Subjunctive PERFECT :   *Me ne sia andáto,* I have gone away.
     PLUPERFECT :   *Me ne fóssi andáto,* I had gone away.

c. Following is a synopsis of the entire passive of *amáre,* " to love " : —

Infinitive PRESENT :   *Êssere amáto,* to be loved.
     PERFECT :   *Êssere státo amáto,* to have been loved.
Participle PRESENT :   *Essèndo amáto,* being loved.
     PERFECT :   *Essèndo státo amáto,* having been loved.
Indicative PRESENT :   *Sóno amáto,* I am loved.
     PERFECT :   *Sóno státo amáto,* I have been loved.
     IMPERFECT :   *Êra amáto,* I was loved.
     PLUPERFECT :   *Êra státo amáto,* I had been loved.
     PRETERITE :   *Fúi amáto,* I was loved.
     PRETERITE PERFECT : *Fúi státo amáto,* I had been loved.
     FUTURE :   *Saró amáto,* I shall be loved.
     FUTURE PERFECT :   *Saró státo amáto,* I shall have been loved.

---

* *Andársene* is composed of the verb *andáre,* " to go," the reflexive *si,* and the adverb *ne,* " thence " (see **47**, *a*).

Conditional: *Sarêi amâto,* I should be loved.
PERFECT: *Sarêi stâto amâto,* I should have been loved.
Imperative: *Sii amâto,* be loved.
Subjunctive PRESENT: *Sia amâto,* I am loved.
PERFECT: *Sia stâto amâto,* I have been loved.
IMPERFECT: *Fôssi amâto,* I were loved.
PLUPERFECT: *Fôssi stâto amâto,* I had been loved.

57. "May" and "can" are generally rendered by *potêre,* "to be able" (see **92,** 21); "must," "should" (expressing duty), and "ought," by *dovêre,* "to owe" (see **92,** 8); "will" (expressing volition) by *volêre,* "to wish" (see **92,** 19).* These verbs are not defective, like the English modal auxiliaries; hence in Italian the tense is expressed by the auxiliary itself, and not by the following infinitive. No preposition intervenes between these verbs and the dependent infinitive.

Ex.: *Può êssere vêro,* it may be true.
Non potêva parlâre, he could not speak.
Hánno potúto dormíre, they have been able to sleep.
Avrêi potúto dírlo, I could have said it.
Potrêmo andâre, we shall be able to go.
Dêve pagârlo, he must pay him.
Dovêmmo veníre, we had to come.
Dovrêbbe fârlo, he should do it, he ought to do it.
Dovrête trovârla, you will have to find her.
Avrêbbe dovúto tacêre, he ought to have kept still.
Vôglio partíre, I will go, I wish to go.
Vorrà tornâre, he will want to return.
Avrêmmo volúto restâre, we should have liked to stay.
Vorrêi sapêre, I should like to know.

---

* "Shall" expressing an order or prohibition is rendered by *dovêre,* by the simple future, or by a phrase consisting of a verb of wishing and a dependent subjunctive: as *non ci andrà,* "he shall not go there"; *dêve capire* or *vôglio che capisca,* "he shall understand."

a. "Must" is also expressed by the impersonal verb *bisognáre*, "to be necessary," followed by the infinitive or by *che*, "that," with the subjunctive. "To have to" is *avére da.*

> Ex.: *Bisógna fárlo*, it must be done.
> *Bisógna che andiámo*, we must go.
> *Ho da scrívere úna léttera*, I have to write a letter.

b. "To be able" meaning "to know how" is *sapére* (see **92**, 6). "Not to be able to help" doing a thing is *non potér a méno di non* (with infinitive) or *non potér fáre a méno di* (with infinitive).

> Ex.: *Non séppe fárlo*, he couldn't do it.
> *Sa léggere e scrívere*, he can read and write.
> *Non potè a méno di non rídere*, he couldn't help laughing.

EXERCISE 13.

Giorgétto è un bambíno víspo, víspo. E sollécito ; álle sêtte è già leváto, ed è già andáto nel giardíno. È mággio, e il giardíno è tútto fioríto ; rôse, gígli, vióle mándano ¹ un odóre soáve. Giorgétto si strúgge ² di cògliere i fióri ; ma la mámma non vuóle ³ : la mámma lo ha lasciáto andár nel giardíno, a pátto che non cogliésse ⁴ i fióri. A un trátto Giorgétto véde ⁵ úna rôsa più bêlla di tútte le áltre, non resíste ⁶ più al desidêrio di pigliárla. La mámma non lo saprà,⁷ non lo può ⁸ sapére, — díce ⁹ fra sè Giorgétto ; e stênde ¹⁰ la máno al cespúglio, ed è per còglierla. Ma che è státo? Ritíra ¹¹ lêsto la máno, e grída,¹² e piánge.¹³ La rôsa ha le spíne : il súo gámbo nascósto tra bellíssime fôglie è tútto piêno di spíne ; e le spíne gli hánno bucáto tútta la máno. La máno è sanguinósa ; e Giorgétto piánge,¹³ e la mámma óra si avvedrà ¹⁴ che il súo bambíno è disobbediênte.

---

¹ Send forth. ² Is dying. ³ Is willing. ⁴ He should pick. ⁵ Sees. ⁶ Resists. ⁷ Will know. ⁸ Can. ⁹ Says. ¹⁰ Stretches out. ¹¹ He draws back. ¹² Screams. ¹³ Cries. ¹⁴ Will see.

EXERCISE 14.

Silvio Pellico was[1] confined in prison; and there, in the silence of his[2] dungeon, he found[3] a friend, a companion — a spider. Yes, a spider made[4] his web in a corner of the prison, and Silvio did[5] not-destroy-it[6]; on-the-contrary,[7] he used-to-throw[8] him crumbs[9] of bread, and little by little he became-so-attached[10] to that spider, and the spider to him, that the creature used-to-come-down[11] from his web and go[12] to find Pellico,[13] and would-go[12] on his[14] hand and take[15] food[9] from his[14] fingers. One day the jailer removed[16] the unhappy Pellico. The prisoner thought-of[17] his spider, and said[18]: "Now that I am-going-away,[19] he will-come-back[20] perhaps, and will-find[21] the prison empty; or if there-is[22] somebody else here,[23] he may[24] be an enemy of spiders,[9] and tear down that beautiful web and crush the poor beast."

[1] Preterite. [2] See **45**, *b*. [3] *Trovò.* [4] *Fèce.* [5] See **54**, *c.* [6] Not to-him it destroyed (*disfèce*). [7] *Anzi.* [8] *Buttáva:* see **54**, *e.* [9] See **13**, *b.* [10] *Tánto si affezionò.* [11] *Si movéva:* see **54**, *e.* [12] *Andáva.* [13] See **13**, *e.* [14] See **45**, *c.* [15] *Prendéva.* [16] *Mutò di stánza.* [17] *Pensáva a.* [18] *Dicéva.* [19] See **54**, *d*, ɩ: *me ne vádo.* [20] *Ritornerà.* [21] *Troverà.* [22] *Vi sarà.* [23] Omit. [24] *Potrèbbe:* see **57.**

REGULAR AND IRREGULAR VERBS.

58. Italian verbs are divided into four conjugations, according as the infinitive ending is *-áre*, accented *-ére*, unaccented *-ere*, or *-ire*. Regular verbs of the second and third conjugations are, however, inflected just alike.

a. The final *e* of the infinitive may be dropped before any word except one beginning with *s* impure.*

* Cf. **10**, *b*; **14**, *b*. Italians find it hard to pronounce three consecutive consonants of which the middle one is *s*.

THE REGULAR VERB.

59. *Parláre,* "to speak," will serve as a model for the first conjugation. All compound tenses are omitted (see 55) : —

Infinitive and Participles.

Parláre, parlándo, parláto.

Indicative.

PRESENT.	IMPERFECT.	PRETERITE.	FUTURE.
Párlo,	*Parláva,*	*Parlái,*	*Parlerò,*
párli,	*parlávi,*	*parlásti,*	*parlerái,*
párla,	*parláva,*	*parlò,*	*parlerà,*
parliámo,	*parlavámo,*	*parlámmo,*	*parlerémo,*
parláte,	*parlaváte,*	*parláste,*	*parleréte,*
párlano.	*parlávano.*	*parlárono.*	*parleránno.*

Imperative.	Subjunctive.		Conditional
	PRESENT.	IMPERFECT.	
	Párli,	*Parlássi,*	*Parleréi,*
Párla,	*párli,*	*parlássi,*	*parlerésti,*
	párli,	*parlásse,*	*parlerèbbe,*
	parliámo,	*parlássimo,*	*parlerémmo,*
	parliáte,	*parláste,*	*parleréste,*
parláte.	*párlino.*	*parlássero.*	*parlerébbero.*

a. Verbs whose infinitives end in *-care* or *-gare* insert *h* after the *c* or *g* in all forms where those letters precede *e* or *i* : as *pághi* (*pagáre*), "let him pay"; *cercherò* (*cercáre*), "I shall search." Verbs in *-ciare* and *-giare* drop the *i* before *e* or *i* : as *mangi* (*mangiáre*), "thou eatest"; *comincerà** (*cominciáre*), "he will

---

* Some writers retain the *i* before *e* : as *comincierà.*

begin." Verbs in -*chiare* and -*gliare* drop the *i* only before another *i*: as *picchi* (*picchiáre*), "let him strike"; *pigli* (*pigliáre*), "thou takest"; but *picchierà, piglierèi*.

b. The verbs *giocáre, rinnováre, rotáre, sonáre* (also written *giuocáre*, etc.) and a few others change *o* of the stem into *uo* in all forms where that vowel is accented: as *suôni*, "let him play"; *giuôcano*, "they play."

60. Verbs of the second and third conjugations * are inflected like *crédere*, "to believe":—

Infinitive and Participles.

Crédere, credêndo, credúto.

Indicative.

PRESENT.	IMPERFECT.	PRETERITE.	FUTURE.
Crédo,	*Credéva,*	*Credéi* (*credétti*),	*Crederò,*
crédi,	*credévi,*	*credésti,*	*crederdi,*
créde,	*credéva,*	*credè* (*credétte*),	*crederà,*
credidmo,	*credevámo,*	*credémmo,*	*crederémo,*
credéte,	*credeváte,*	*credéste,*	*crederéte,*
crédono.	*credévano.*	*credérono* (*credéttero*).	*crederánno.*

Imperative.	Subjunctive.		Conditional.
	PRESENT.	IMPERFECT.	
	Créda,	*Credéssi,*	*Crederéi,*
Crédi,	*créda,*	*credéssi,*	*crederésti,*
	créda,	*credésse,*	*crederébbe,*
	credidmo,	*credéssimo,*	*crederémmo,*
credéte.	*credidte,*	*credéste,*	*crederéste,*
	crédano.	*credéssero.*	*crederébbero.*

* Most grammars and dictionaries class these two together as the "second conjugation."

Báttere, compétere, convérgere, divérgere, méscere, miétere, páscere, prescéndere, rifléttere, ripétere, téssere, tóndere, and their compounds do not have in the preterite the forms in parentheses. Verbs in *-cere* and *-gere* insert after the *c* or *g* an *i* before *u*, but not before any other vowel: *méscere, mésco, mésca, mesciúto.*

61. Most verbs of the fourth conjugation * are inflected like *finíre,* "to finish" : —

Infinitive and Participles.

Finire,　　　　*finéndo,*　　　　*finito.*

Indicative.

PRESENT.	IMPERFECT.	PRETERITE.	FUTURE.
Finisco,	*Finiva,*	*Finii,*	*Finirò,*
finisci,	*finivi,*	*finisti,*	*finirdi,*
finisce,	*finiva,*	*finì,*	*finirà,*
finidmo,	*finivdmo,*	*finimmo,*	*finirémo,*
finite,	*finivdte,*	*finiste,*	*finiréte,*
finiscono.	*finivano.*	*finirono.*	*finirdnno.*

Imperative.	Subjunctive.		Conditional.
	PRESENT.	IMPERFECT.	
	Finisca,	*Finissi,*	*Finirêi,*
Finisci,	*finisca,*	*finissi,*	*finirésti,*
	finisca,	*finisse,*	*finirêbbe,*
	finidmo,	*finissimo,*	*finirémmo,*
finite.	*finidte,*	*finiste,*	*finiréste,*
	finiscano.	*finissero.*	*finirêbbero.*

But *aborríre,† assorbíre,† avvertíre, bollíre, divertíre, dormíre, fuggíre,‡ mentíre,† partíre,† pentíre, pervertíre, sentíre, servíre, sortíre,† tossíre,† vestíre,* and their compounds,

---

* Most grammars and dictionaries call this the "third conjugation."

† *Aborrire, assorbire, mentire, sortire, tossire* may also follow *finire. Partire,* "to distribute," is like *finire; partire,* "to depart," like *sentire.*

‡ *Fuggire* does not insert *i: fúggo, fúgga.*

though inflected like *finíre* in all other parts, are in the present indicative, imperative, and subjunctive conjugated after the following model : —

Indicative.	Imperative.	Subjunctive.
Sènto,		*Sènta,*
sènti,	*Sènti,*	*sènta,*
sènte,		*sènta,*
sentidmo,		*sentidmo,*
sentite,	*sentite.*	*sentidte,*
sèntono.		*sèntano.*

62. The present participle of all verbs is invariable.

63. In all conjugations a form of the first person singular of the imperfect indicative ending in *o* instead of *a* is often used in conversation : as *leggévo,* " I was reading." Final *o* of the third person plural of the various tenses is frequently omitted : as *vèngon da me,* " they come to me."

a. In the preterite *-no* is occasionally dropped, especially in poetry : as *parláro,* " they spoke." Final *o* of the first person plural of the present subjunctive is sometimes omitted in poetry : as *andiàm,* " let us go."

b. In old Italian, in poetry, and in some modern prose *v* of the imperfect indicative is sometimes omitted in verbs of the second, third, and fourth conjugations, but only in the first and third persons singular and the third person plural : as *lo avéano fátto,* " they had done it."

c. In old Italian and in poetry the conditional endings *-èi,* *-èbbe,* *-èbbero* are often replaced by *-ia,* *-ia,* *-iano :* as *crederia,* " he would believe."

d. In old Italian and in poetry the third person plural ending *-ero* is sometimes replaced by *-ono :* as *avrèbbono,* " they would have" ; *che andássono,* " that they should go."

THE IRREGULAR VERB.

64. Certain parts of Italian irregular verbs are always regular : the example given below will show which they are. *Èssere* (see 53, *a*) is an exception to all rules.

65. Many irregular verbs that belong or once belonged to the third conjugation have the infinitive contracted (*fáre* for *fácere, díre* for *dícere, condúrre* for *condúcere*) : in this case the future and conditional are formed from this contracted infinitive (*faró, diréi, condurrébbe*), while the present participle, the imperfect indicative and subjunctive, and certain persons of the present and preterite are formed from the uncontracted stem (*facêndo, dicéva, conduciámo*).

66. *Pórre* (for *pónere*), "to put," a verb of the third conjugation, will serve to show which are the regular and which the irregular parts of irregular verbs : the forms printed in italics are regular in all verbs except *dáre, díre, èssere, fáre, stáre;* those in Roman type may be irregular.

Infinitive and Participles.

| Pórre, | *ponêndo,* | pósto. |

Indicative.

PRESENT.	IMPERFECT.	PRETERITE.	FUTURE.
Póngo,	*Ponéva,*	Pósi,	Porró,
póni,	*ponévi,*	*ponésti,*†	porrái,
póne,	*ponéva,*	póse,	porrà,
poniámo,	*ponevámo,*	*ponémmo,*†	porrémo,
*ponéte,**	*poneváte,*	*ponéste,*†	porréte,
póngono.	*ponévano.*	pósero.	porránno.

* See **66**, 4.   † See **66**, 3.

Imperative.	Subjunctive.		Conditional.
	PRESENT.	IMPERFECT.	
	Pónga,	*l'onéssi,* *	Porrêi,
Póni,	pónga,	*ponéssi,*	porrésti,
	pónga,	*ponésse,*	porrêbbe,
	poniámo,	*ponéssimo,*	porrémmo,
ponéte.	poniáte,	*ponéste,*	porréste,
	póngano.	*ponéssero.*	porrêbbero.

It will be seen that the present participle, the imperfect indicative and subjunctive, and certain persons of the present and preterite indicative are always regular.

(1) *Dáre* and *stáre* have in the future and conditional *darò, darêi; starò, starêi.* Otherwise the only irregularity in the future and conditional is that they are contracted in many verbs even when the infinitive is uncontracted: as *vedére,* "to see," *vedrò; veníre,* "to come," *verrêi.*

(2) From the first person singular of the preterite the other irregular persons can be constructed, the third person singular by changing the ending *i* to *e*, the third person plural by adding *-ro* to the third person singular.†

(3) The *regular* persons of the preterite and the whole imperfect subjunctive are slightly irregular in *dáre* and *stáre,* which substitute *e* for *a* in those forms (*désti, démmo, déste, déssi; stésti, stémmo, stéste, stéssi*).

(4) *Díre* (for *dícere*) and *fáre* (for *fácere*) have irregular forms, *díte* and *fáte,* in the second person plural of the present indicative.

a. It may be well to note that the first person plural of the present indicative, and first and second persons plural of the

---

* See 66, 3.
† This rule applies only to *irregular* preterites.

present subjunctive are irregular only in *avére, dolére, dovére, fáre, giacére, piacére, potére, sapére, solére, tacére, valére, volére.* In *fáre* (for *fácere*), *giacére, piacére,* and *tacére* the irregularity consists in doubling the *c* before *ia;* *sapére* doubles the *p;* *dolére, solére, valére,* and *volére* substitute *glia* for *lia.* In *avére, dovére,* and *potére* the stem is changed : *abbiámo, abbiáte; dobbiámo, dobbiáte; possiámo, possiáte.*

b. The two persons of the imperative are exactly like the corresponding persons of the present indicative, except in *avére, sapére,* and *volére,* where they follow the subjunctive (*ábbi, abbiáte; sáppi, sappiáte; vógli, vogliáte*), and in *andáre, dáre, díre, fáre,* and *stáre,* which have in the singular *va', da', di, fa', sta'.*

c. The third person plural of the present indicative can always be constructed from the first person singular, from which can be formed also the whole present subjunctive except the first and second persons plural : these come from the first person plural of the present indicative. Exceptions to this rule are *andáre, avére, dáre, fáre, sapére,* and *stáre,* which have in the third person plural of the present indicative *vánno, hánno, dánno, fánno, sánno, stánno;* while *avére, dáre, sapére,* and *stáre* have in the present subjunctive *ábbia, día, sáppia, stía.*

67. With the aid of the above notes any verb except *éssere* can be constructed from the infinitive, the participles (the present participle often being necessary to show the uncontracted form of the infinitive), the singular of the present indicative, and the first person singular of the preterite and future.

a. In poetry and in some prose works *ggi* is often substituted for *d* in the present of verbs in -*dere:* as *chiéggio = chiédo,* " I ask " ; *véggia = véda,* " let him see."

b. In old Italian we find *fóro* for *fúrono, fóra* for *saréi* or *sarébbe, fórano* for *sarébbero, fía* for *sarà,* and *fíano* for *saránno.*

c. Verbs whose stem ends in *l, n,* or *r* may drop the final vowel in the second and third persons singular of the present indicative, and in the imperative singular : as *vien qui,* "come here " ; *non par possibile,* " it doesn't seem possible " ; *non vuol andáre,* " he won't go."

d. See **68,** *a, b, c, d.*

68. At the end of the book (page 88) will be found a list of irregular verbs. There all irregular parts will be printed in full, except the preterite and (contracted) future, of which the first person singular will be given. The conditional, which is always formed from the same stem as the future, will not be mentioned. The imperative will be given only when it differs from the present indicative.

a. In general, compound verbs will not be included in this list : those differing in conjugation from their simple verbs will be given in the Alphabetical List of Irregular and Defective Verbs (page 100). All compounds of *dáre* and *fáre* are accented on the same syllable as the simple verbs : as *fa,* "he does " ; *disfà,* " he undoes."

The compounds of *stáre* demand special mention : *ristáre, soprastáre, sottostáre, sovrastáre,* are inflected like *stáre (ristà, soprastétti, sottostíano) ; distáre* has no present participle, is regular in the present of all moods (*dísto,* etc.), but otherwise is inflected like *stáre (distétti,* etc.) ; *constáre, contrastáre, instáre, ostáre, restáre, sostáre* are regular throughout (*cónsta, contrástano, instái, ostárono, rèsti, sostássi*).

EXERCISE 15.

Tánto all' andáre quánto al tornáre dálla scuôla, Enríco dà[1] nôia a tútti ; picchia i bambíni più piccíni di lúi, tíra i sássi a quálche pôvero cáne che se ne va[2] tranquillaménte pel súo viággio, rómpe le piánte del giardíno che dève[3] traversáre per andáre a scuôla o per tornáre a cása ; insómma è un contínuo far malánni.

Il bábbo va[2] a lavoráre la mattína présto; la mámma è maláta, e
quíndi non lo póssono[4] accompagnáre. L' áltra mattína però gli
• seguì brútta. Méntre andáva a scuòla, víde[5] avánti a sè un bambíno piccíno, tútto vestíto bène, e che paréva sólo; Enríco, sènza
far tánti discórsi, arríva di diètro, gli píglia il cappèllo e gliélo
bútta in úna fónte che èra lì vicína. Il póvero bambíno si métte
a piángere, e Enríco cominciò a scappáre. Ma quésta vôlta avéva
fátto[6] mále i suôi cónti: il bambíno non èra sólo, lo accom-
pagnáva un bel can barbóne. I can barbóni hánno tánto intendiménto, che fánno[6] áltre côse ben più meraviglióse che andáre
ad accompagnáre a scuòla un bambíno. Il barbóne dúnque, cóme
víde[5] il súo padroncíno assalíto, vía diètro ad Enríco che fuggíva;
in un áttimo lo raggiúnse,[7] e agguantátagli úna gámba, lo badáva
a môrdere[8]; Enríco urláva, ma il cáne non lo lasciò finchè un
signóre, che avéva vísto[5] tútta la scèna, non lo minacciò col bastóne. Enríco èbbe stracciáti i calzóni, laceráta la cárne délla
gámba, e fu pôi puníto dal maèstro e dái genitóri; ma da quel
giórno a quésta párte non dà[1] più nôia a nessúno, avèndo vedúto
che un cáne stésso gli avéva insegnáto cóme fósse mále molestáre
gli áltri.

[1] From _dáre_, **92**, 3.   [2] _Andáre, andársene_, **92**, 1.   [3] _Dovére_, **92**, 8.   [4] _Po-
tére_, **92**, 21.   [5] _Vedére_, **92**, 10.   [6] _Fáre_, **92**, 2.   [7] _Raggiúngere_, **92**, 89.
[8] He kept biting him.

EXERCISE 16.

Have you ever observed what[1] happens when a pot of water
boils at the fire? The steam of the water rises like so-much
smoke, and remains attached to the lid that covers the pot; when
this steam has begun to cool, it becomes[2] water once-more,[2] and
falls[3] down again[3] drop by drop. In-like-manner[4] it happens
with[5] the vapors which the sun and the heat lift from the earth.
The vapors rise, collect themselves on[6] high in little bubbles, and
thus united they form clouds.[7] When these clouds are very-much[8]
charged with[9] moisture, they resolve themselves into water; and

the water, falling[3] down again[3] in drops where the wind carries it, forms rain.[7] So[10] rain[7] is-only[11] steam turned-back-into[12] water. The cloud, too,[13] is-only[11] a quantity of steam not-very[14] dense and not-very[14] high[15] in the air. This vapor, by[16] remaining low, prevents us sometimes from-seeing[17] objects[7] even at a[16] small distance from us.

[1] *Quéllo che.* [2] To become once more = *ritornáre.* [3] To fall again = *ricascáre.* [4] *Medesimaménte.* [5] *Per.* [6] *In.* [7] See **13**, *b.* [8] *Mólto.* [9] *Di.* [10] *Dúnque.* [11] *Non è áltro che.* [12] *Tornáto.* [13] *Pói.* [14] *Póco.* [15] *Solleváto.* [16] Omit. [17] *Di vedére.*

MOODS AND TENSES.

69. The English present participle used as subject or direct object of a verb must be rendered in Italian by the infinitive, nearly always with the article *il.*

> Ex.: *Mi piáce il viaggiáre,* I like travelling.
> *La nòstra prima cúra fu il cercáre úna pensióne,* our first care was hunting up a boarding-house.
> *Rifársela cógli animáli è da sciòcchi,* taking vengeance on animals is folly.

70. The English present participle preceded by a preposition is translated as follows : (1) If in English the preposition can be omitted without essentially changing the sense (even though the construction be awkward), the phrase is rendered in Italian by the present participle without any preposition.

It is, however, to be noted that " to amuse one's self by . . .," "to weary one's self by . . ." are *divertirsi a . . ., affannársi a . . .* with the infinitive. A few other verbs take this same construction.

(2) If the preposition is a necessary part of the thought, it is expressed in Italian, and the English present participle is rendered by the infinitive with the article *il*. This article is, however, always omitted after the prepositions "after" (*dópo di*), "before" (*prima di*), "instead of" (*invéce di*), "without" (*sénza*); and also after "of" (*di*) when in English the present participle cannot be replaced by a noun.

> Ex.: *Studiándo si impára*, (through) studying we learn.
>
> *Dovréi corrispóndere álla súa cortesía ascoltándola*, I ought to acknowledge her courtesy (by) listening to her.
>
> *Partèndo incontrò un amíco*, (on) going away he met a friend.
>
> *Copiándo non fa erróri*, (in) copying he makes no mistakes.
>
> *Si divèrte a tirár sássi*, he amuses himself (by) throwing stones.
>
> *Óltre il fáre scarabócchi scríve mále*, **besides** making blots he writes badly.
>
> *Parlái cóntra il tràrre útile di quélla disgrázia*, I spoke **against** utilizing that misfortune.
>
> *Prima di morire*, **before** dying.
>
> *Invéce di dírmi tútto*, **instead of** telling me everything.
>
> *Parliámo sénza riflèttere*, we speak **without** thinking.
>
> *Quésta vittória fu cagióne del sostituíre un magistráto déi Nòve a quéllo déi Trénta*, this victory was the cause **of** the substituting (= substitution of) a magistracy of the Nine for that of the Thirty.
>
> *Ho l' abitúdine di coricármi tárdi*, I am in the habit **of** going to bed late.
>
> *Il vízio di fumáre*, the habit **of** smoking.

71. Following are some other rules for the use of the infinitive and participles : —

a. When any verb is used as an auxiliary, the mood and tense are expressed in that verb, and not in the dependent infinitive (see **57**).

> Ex.: *Avréi potúto fárlo*, I could have done it.

b. After *fáre*, "to make" or "to have" (= "to cause"), *sentire* and *udíre*, "to hear," and *vedére*, "to see," the Italian present infinitive is used to render an English past participle. After *lasciáre*, "to let," and often after the preposition *da* an Italian active infinitive is used to translate a passive one in English.

> Ex.: *Si fa capíre*, he makes himself understood.
> *Farò fáre un páio di scárpe*, I shall have a pair of shoes made.
> *L' ho sentito díre*, I have heard it said.
> *Lo víde ammazzáre*, he saw him killed.
> *Si láscia ingannáre*, he lets himself be deceived.
> *Non c' è niènte da fáre*, there is nothing to be done.

c. The Italian past participle is inflected like any other adjective. The present participle is invariable. When in English the present participle is used adjectively, without any verbal force whatsoever, it is translated, not by the participle, but by a verbal adjective, which can be formed from almost any Italian verb by changing the infinitive ending into *-ánte* for the first conjugation, and into *-ènte* for the others. This adjective may be used substantively.

> Ex.: *Quésti vási sóno rótti*, these vases are broken.
> *La dónna sta cucèndo*, the woman is sewing.
> *Un animále parlánte*, a speaking animal.
> *Díe amánti*, two lovers.

d. A whole protasis is often expressed in Italian by a present participle, or by an infinitive with *a*.

> Ex.: *Andándovi lo vedrèbbe*, if he went there, he would see it.
> *A bucársi ésce il sángue*, if you prick yourself, blood comes.

e. A clause in indirect discourse is sometimes replaced by the infinitive followed by the subject.

> Ex.: *Disse èssere quésto l' uómo che cercavámo*, he said this was the man we were looking for.

72. In negative commands the infinitive is always used instead of the second person singular of the imperative.

Ex.: *Tròvalo*, find it; *non lo trovàre*, do not find it.

73. When an action is represented as having taken place and still continuing, the English uses the perfect or pluperfect tense, the Italian the present or imperfect.

Ex.: *Stúdio l' italiáno da ôtto mési*, I have studied Italian for eight months.

74. In subordinate clauses referring to the future and introduced by a conjunction of time, where the present is often used in English, the future tense must be employed in Italian.

Ex.: *Quándo vi andrò, gliélo dirò*, when I go there, I'll tell him.

a. The future is often used, without any idea of future time, to express probability.

Ex.: *Sarà usclto*, he has probably gone out.
Avrà mólto denáro, he probably has a great deal of money.

75. The difference between the imperfect and the preterite is this: the preterite is used of an event that occurred at a definite date in the past, the imperfect is used in a description or in speaking of an accessory circumstance or an habitual action in past time — the preterite is a narrative, the imperfect a descriptive tense. The preterite perfect is used (instead of the pluperfect) only after conjunctions meaning "as soon as" (*appéna che, súbito che, tôsto che*), and sometimes after *dópo che*, "after."*

* It is used also in phrases like: *in cinque minúti ébbe finíta la léttera*, "in five minutes he had the letter finished."

Ex.: *Entrò mèntre dormivàmo*, he came in while we slept.
Facèvo così ógni mattina, I did so every morning.
Lo féce l' ánno scórso, he did it last year.
Tòsto che l' èbbe vìsto, uscì, as soon as he had seen it, he went.

a. In conversation the perfect is often used instead of the preterite, when the event is not remote.

Ex.: *Vi sóno andàto ièri*, I went there yesterday.

76. The conditional, like the English "should" and "would," has two uses: in indirect discourse after a principal verb in a past tense it expresses the tense which in direct discourse would be future;* in the conclusion of a conditional sentence it is used when the protasis is (or, if expressed, would be) in the imperfect subjunctive (see **77**).

Ex.: *Dísse che lo farèbbe*, he said he would do it.
Se fòsse véro lo crederéi, if it were true, I should believe it.
Quésta càsa mi converrèbbe, this house would suit me.

77. When a condition is contrary to fact, or consists of a more or less unlikely supposition referring to future time,† the protasis is in the imperfect (or pluperfect) subjunctive, the apodosis in the conditional;‡ otherwise both protasis and apodosis are in the indicative.

Ex.: *Se l' avèssi te lo daréi*, if I had it, I should give it thee.
Se fòsse tornàto l' avrèi vedùto, if he had returned, I should have seen him.
Se venísse nòi ce ne andrèmmo, if he came, we should go.
Se vi andàssi morréi, if I should go there, I should die.

---

* The perfect conditional is sometimes used where the simple tense would be expected: *disse che non l' avrèbbe fàtto più*, "he said he would do it no more."

† Rendered in English by the imperfect, or by the auxiliary "should."

‡ The imperfect indicative is occasionally used to replace the imperfect or pluperfect subjunctive of the protasis and the conditional of the apodosis.

Se non è véro è ben trováto, if it isn't true, it's a good invention.
Se lo féce sarà puníto, if he did it, he will be punished.

a. The missing persons of the imperative are supplied from the present subjunctive. The imperfect subjunctive is used to express a wish that is not likely to be realized.

Ex. : *La si régoli,* moderate yourself; *si accòmodi.* be seated.
Stíano zítti, be quiet (pl.) : *andiámo,* let us go.
Sia púre, be it so ; *véngano súbito,* let them come at once.
Fósse púre, would it were so.

b. When a relative clause restricts its antecedent to one of all its possible conditions or actions, the verb of that relative clause is in the subjunctive, — the present subjunctive if the verb on which it depends be present or future, the imperfect if it be past or conditional.

Ex.: *Non c' è animále più bellíno d' un gátto gióvane che fáccia il chiásso,* there is no animal prettier than a kitten that is at play.
Dóve troveríte un gióvine che spósi vói, where will you find a young man who will marry *you ?*
Vorrèi vedére un bel quádro che non fósse antíco, I should like to see a fine picture that is not old.

c. The verb of a subordinate clause depending on an impersonal verb, on a superlative, or on one of the words "first," "last," and "only" is in the subjunctive. But the indicative is used after an affirmative phrase meaning "it is true" or " it is because."

Ex.: *Bisognò ch' io vi andássi,* I had to go there.
È giústo che stano puníti, it's right they should be punished.
E il più piccolo animále che esísta, it's the smallest animal that exists.
È véro che ci sóno státo, it's true that I've been there.

d. The subjunctive is used after all conjunctions meaning "although," "as if," "unless," "provided that," "in order that," "in such a way that" (denoting purpose), "before," "however," "whenever," "wherever," "without."

Ex.: *Benchè stia nascósto, lo troverò, dovúnque stia,* although he be
hidden, I shall find him, wherever he is.

Partirò a méno che égli non vènga, I shall go unless he
comes.

Lo féce perchè io venissi, he did it that I might come.

La divise in mòdo che le due párti fóssero ugudli, he divided it
in such a way that the two parts should be equal.

Per quánto ricco égli sia, however rich he may be.

Aspétta finchè io tórni, wait until I return.

e. The subjunctive is used after the indefinite pronouns *quále
che, qualúnque, chiúnque, checchè, per quánto.*

Ex.: *Chiúnque vènga,* whoever comes.

Qualúnque disgrázia che succèda, whatever misfortune happens.

Per quánte vòlte ci váda, however many times I go there.

f. The verb of an indirect question is nearly always in the
subjunctive when it depends on a main verb either in a past tense
or in the conditional.

Ex.: *Domándano se il re è mórto,* they ask whether the king is
dead.

Domandò se il pádre fósse uscito, he asked whether his father
was out.

g. In a clause dependent on a verb of saying the subjunctive
is used if the main verb is negative, or interrogative, or in the
conditional, or in a past tense. It is generally not used, however,
after an affirmative verb in a past tense when the author himself
wishes to imply that the indirect statement is true.

Ex.: *Dice che la còsa è chiaríssima,* he says the thing is perfectly
clear.

Non dico che quésto sia véro, I don't say this is true.

Dissero che lo zio fósse ammaláto, they said their uncle
was ill.

Gli dissi che mi chiamáva Enrico, I told him my name was
Henry.

h. The subjunctive is used after verbs expressing causation, concession, desire, emotion, prevention, and uncertainty : *i.e.*, after verbs of bringing about ; granting, permitting ; commanding, hoping, requesting, wishing ; fearing, regretting, rejoicing ; forbidding, hindering ; being ignorant, denying, disbelieving, doubting, expecting, pretending, supposing, suspecting, thinking.

> Ex.: *Non so chi siano*, I don't know who they are.
>
> *Vorrèi che quésto non fósse accadúto*, I wish this had not happened.
>
> *Supponidmo che sia prováto*, let us suppose that it is proved.
>
> *Spéro mi scriva prèsto*, I hope you will write to me soon.

i. Se, "if," is occasionally omitted before an imperfect subjunctive ; in this case the subject, if expressed, must follow the verb.

> Ex.: *Sarêi felice venísse égli*, I should be happy, should he come.

EXERCISE 17.

La mámma di Alfrédo avéva lasciáto un anêllo d' ôro sul cassettóne. Alfrédo vôlle[1] métterselo in díto. Che giudízio ! pretêndere che l' anêllo délla mámma pôssa[2] stáre in un ditíno d' un fanciúllo ! Se lo míse[3] nel díto grôsso e pôi s' affacció álla finêstra ; l' anêllo cascó di sótto, e non se ne sêppe[4] piú núlla. La mámma cérca l' anêllo, ma non c' êra più ; cérca di qui, di là, di sópra, cérca per tútto, nè l' anêllo si può[2] trováre. Allóra chiáma Alfrédo e gli dice[5] : — Bambíno, dímmi[6] la verità ; hái préso[7] tu il mio anêllo? l' hái pêrso[8] tu? — Alfrédo, cattívo, disse[5] di no. La mámma si ricordáva bêne d' avérlo lasciáto nel vassoíno sul cassettóne. Non credéva Alfrédo capáce di dir le bugíe, quíndi sospettó che qualcúno l' avésse rubáto. Ci andáva in cása[9] úna bambína, figliuôla d' un antíco súo servitóre, e il sospêtto cádde[10] sópra quésta pôvera creatúra. La mámma di Alfrédo non la vôlle[1] più in cása ; ma l' allontanó con bêlla maniêra, e nessúno si avvíde[11] di núlla, perchè quélla signóra êra buôna. Peró la bugía di Alfrédo féce[12] si che súa mádre credésse ládra quélla pôvera bambina. Dio perdóni Alfrédo, Dio gl' ispíri di rimediáre a si brútta azióne ; váda,[13] si bútti ái piédi délla mámma, le raccónti tútto, e non commétta mái più di quéste azionácce.

[1] From volére, 92, 19.   [2] Potére, 92, 21.   [3] Méttere, 92, 104.   [4] Sapére, 92, 6.   [5] Dire, 92, 152.   [6] Dire: see 48, d.   [7] Préndere, 92, 47.   [8] Pérdere, 92, 46.   [9] There used to come to the house.   [10] Cadére, 92, 7.   [11] Avvedérsi, 92, 10.   [12] Fáre, 92, 2.   [13] Andáre, 92, 1.

EXERCISE 18.

We inhabit the earth ; but not all the earth has the same name everywhere : the earth is-divided[1] into five parts, and every part has its name. The five parts of the earth are-called[1] : Europe, Asia, Africa, America, Oceanica. Imagine you-cut-open[2] the earth in the middle and place[3] it on a table, in-such-a-way[4] that the inside shall-rest[5] on the table, and the outside shall-present[5] itself to your eyes. You will have two circles : in the circle that lies[6] at your right are[7] Europe, Asia, Africa, and a part of Oceanica ; in the circle that lies[6] on-the[8] left are[7] America and the other part of Oceanica. But the ancients did[9] not[10] believe that the earth was round, nor did[9] they know that its parts were five. They thought that the earth was flat and surrounded by the sea ; they knew, moreover,[11] only[12] three parts : Europe, Asia, Africa.   They never[13] would have dreamed that the earth was round, and that on[14] the side opposite to the-one[15] which they inhabited there[16] was inhabited land. America was discovered 395 years ago by an Italian who was-called[1] Christopher Columbus. Christopher Columbus was-born[17] in a village near Genoa in 1447. His parents were poor ; his father earned hardly enough-to[14] support the family. However, by-dint[18] of sacrifices they had[19] him study ; and as[20] Christopher studied willingly, he grew up a fine[21] boy. When it was time[22] to-choose[23] a profession, he chose to-be-a[24] sailor.   In[8] those times they believed that the world ended

after Africa ; but Columbus, on-the-contrary,[25] persuaded himself
that the world ought[26] not[10] to[26] end there, and that by continuing
to sail, one[1] ought[26] to[26] turn and come-back to the same point.

[1] See **54**, *g.*   [2] *Di aprire.*   [3] *Di posdre.*   [4] *In môdo.*   [5] See **77**, *d.*   [6] Use
restdre.   [7] *C' è.*   [8] *A.*   [9] See **54**, *c.*   [10] *Non,* "not," must precede the
verb.   [11] *Pôi.*   [12] See **82**.   [13] See **83**.   [14] *Da.*   [15] *Quélla.*   [16] *Vi.*
[17] To be born = *ndscere,* **92**, 128.   [18] *A fôrza.*   [19] Use *fdre,* **92**, 2.
[20] *Perchè.*   [21] *Brdvo.*   [22] Use def. article.   [23] *Di scégliere.*   [24] *Di fdre*
il.   [25] *Invéce.*   [26] See **57**.

CONJUNCTIONS, PREPOSITIONS, AND ADVERBS.

CONJUNCTIONS.

78. The principal conjunctions are : —

After, *dôpo che.*

Also, *dnche, púre.*

Although, *benchè, sebbéne, non ostdnte*
che.

And, *e.*

As, *côme, qudnto* (after *tdnto*).

As (= since), *siccôme, poichè.*

As fast as, *via via che.*

As if, *côme se, qudsi.*

As long as, *finchè.*

As well as, *côme dnco.*

Because, *perchè.*

Before, *prima che, avdnti che.*

Both . . . and, *e . . . e.*

But, *ma.*

Either . . . or, *o . . . o.*

Even if, *dnche se, ancorchè.*

Except that, *se non che.*

For, *chè.*

Granting that, *ddto che.*

However (= nevertheless), *però, púre.*

However (before an adj.), *qualúnque,*
per qudnto.

If, *se.*

In case, *cdso.*

In order that, *perchè, acciochè, affinchè.*

Much less, *non che.*

Neither . . . nor, *nè . . . nè.*

Nevertheless, *tuttavia, nondiméno, però.*

Nor, *nè, nemméno, neppúre.*

Nor . . . either, *nemméno, neppúre.*

Nor even, *nednche, neppúre.*

Not to say . . . but even, *non che . . . ma*

Or, *o, ovvéro, ossia.*

Or else, *ossia.*

Provided that, *purchè.*

Rather, *dnzi.*

Since (temporal), *dacchè.*

Since (causal), *poichè, siccòme.*
So, *dúnque, adúnque.*
So that (result), *di mòdo che, sicchè.*
So that (= in order that), *perchè.*
Than, *che.*
That, *che.*
That (= in order that), *perchè.*
Then, *dúnque.*
Therefore, *dúnque, però, perciò, adúnque*
  (at the beginning of a clause).

Too, *púre, ánche.*
Unless, *a mèno che non, eccètto che non, sènza che.*
Until, *finchè non.*
When, *quándo.*
Whence, *dónde.*
Where, *dòve, òve, là dòve.*
Wherever, *dovúnque.*
Whether, *se.*
While, *méntre, méntre che.*

The final vowel of *ánche, che, dòve, neppúre,* and *òve* is generally elided before *e* or *i.*

a. Of the above conjunctions *acciochè, affinchè, a mèno che non, ancorchè, avánti che, benchè, cáso, cóme se, dáto che, dovúnque, eccètto che non, non ostánte che, perchè* meaning "in order that," *per quánto, prima che, purchè, qualúnque, quási, sebbène,* and *sènza che* are followed by the subjunctive. For the use of *che,* "that," with the subjunctive, see **77,** *c, g, h. Cóme* is occasionally used for *cóme se,* and then it takes the subjunctive. *Finchè* when referring to the future sometimes has the sense of *finchè non,* and then it generally takes the subjunctive. *Se* is followed by the subjunctive when it introduces an indirect question dependent on a verb in a past tense, or a condition contrary to fact. For examples, see **77,** *c, d, f, g, h.*

b. Che cannot be omitted in Italian as "that" is in English :* as *disse che fósse véro,* "he said it was true." *Se* can be omitted in a condition contrary to fact : as *fóssi ricco saréi felice,* "were I rich, I should be happy."

---

* It is omitted, however, in the following peculiarly Italian construction : *il ragázzo paréva fósse felice,* "the boy seemed to be happy"; that is, between a verb of seeming and the subjunctive dependent on it, when in English the construction would be a verb of seeming with a dependent infinitive. It is occasionally omitted also after verbs of wishing, hoping, and fearing : as *spéro mi scriva présto,* "I hope you will write to me soon."

c. *E* and *o* are often written *ed* and *od* before a vowel.

Ex.: *Mio pádre ed io*, my father and I.

d. Between a verb of motion and an infinitive "and" is rendered by the preposition *a*.

Ex.: *Andrò a cercárlo*, I'll go and look for it.

e. When *ánche*, "also" or "too," relates to a personal pronoun, the disjunctive form of that pronoun must follow *ánche*, even if some form of the same pronoun has already been expressed.

Ex.: *Andrémo ánche nói*, we shall go too.
Párte anch' égli, he goes away too.
Trovái ánche lúi, I found him too.
Vénnero anch' éssi, they came too.
Lo or *me lo diéde anche a me*, he gave it to me too.
Ti piáce ánche a te, you like it too.

PREPOSITIONS.

79. The principal prepositions are:—

About (= approximately), *circa*.
About (= around), *intórno a, attórno a*.
Above, *sópra*.
According to, *secóndo*.
After, *dópo, dópo di*.
Against, *cóntra, cóntro*.
Along, *lúngo*.
Among, *fra, tra*.
Around, *intórno a, attórno a*.
As far as, *fíno a, síno a*.
As for, *per, quánto a, in quánto a*.
As to, *rispétto a*.
At, *a*.
Because of, *per motívo di*.
Before (time), *prima di, innánzi*.

Before (place), *davánti a, innánzi*.
Behind, *diétro*.
Below, *sótto*.
Beside (place), *accánto a*.
Besides, beside (= in addition to), *óltre*.
Between, *fra, tra*.
Beyond, *óltre, al di là di*.
By, *da, accánto a* (= beside).
By means of, *per mézzo di*.
During, *duránte*.
Except, *tránne, eccétto, fuóri di*.
For, *per*.
From, *da, fin da*.
In, *in*.
In front of, *davánti a, innánzi*.

Inside of, *déntro di*.	Round and round, *tórno tórno a*.
Instead of, *invéce di*.	Since, *da*.
In the midst of, *in mézzo a*.	To, *a*.
Into, *in*.	Toward, *vérso*.
Near, *vicino a*.	Through, *per*.
Of, *di*.	Under, *sótto*.
On, *su* (before a vowel, *sur*), *sópra*.	Upon, *su* (before vowels, *sur*), *sópra*.
On this side of, *al di quà di*.	Up to, *fino a, sino a*.
On to, *su* (before vowels, *sur*), *sópra*.	With, *con*.
Opposite, *dirimpétto a*.	Within, *fra, tra*.
Out of, *da, di, fuóri di*.	Within (= inside of), *déntro di*.
Outside of, *fuóri di*.	Without, *sénza*.
Over, *sópra*.	Without (= outside of), *fuóri di*.

When governing a personal pronoun *cóntra, diétro, dópo, sénza, sópra, sótto*, and often *fra* and *vérso* take *di* after them : as *sénza di me,* "without me" ; *fra di lóro,* "among themselves." After *con, in, per,* a word beginning with *s* impure generally prefixes *i*[*] : as *la stráda,* "the street " ; *in istráda,* "in the street."

a. "To " before the name of a country, after a verb of motion, is *in*.

Ex. : *Andiámo in Fráncia,* let us go to France.

b. "To " before an infinitive is rendered in Italian as follows : (1) After the verbs *bastáre,* "suffice" ; *bisognáre,* "need " ; *conveníre,* "suit" ; *desideráre,* "desire " ; *dovére,* "must," "ought " ; *fáre,* "make " ; *lasciáre,* "let " ; *parére,* "seem " ; *potére,* "can," "be able" ; *sapére,* "know " ; *sentíre,* "hear," "feel " ; *solére,* "be accustomed" ; *udíre,* "hear " ; *vedére,* "see " ; and *volére,* "wish," "to " before a following infinitive is omitted. It is omitted also in exclamations and indirect questions consisting only of an interrogative and an infinitive.

---

[*] Cf. **58**, *a*.

Ex.: *Dovrèi capíre*, I ought to understand.
Bisógna pensárci, it is necessary to look out for it.
Potrémo veníre, we shall be able to come.
Vorrèi sapére, I should like to know.
Non sa che fáre nè dóve avvólgersi, he doesn't know what to do nor where to turn.

(2) After verbs of accustoming, attaining, beginning, compelling, continuing, helping, learning, teaching, and after verbs of motion, "to" before a following infinitive is *a*.

Ex.: *Andránno a vedérla*, they will go to see her.
Si affrettò a rispóndere, he hastened to reply.

(3) After all other verbs it is *di;* but "to" denoting purpose or result is *per*, and "to" indicating duty or necessity is *da*.

Ex.: *Gli díssi di scrívere*, I told him to write.
Mi è gráto di dírlo, I am happy to say so.
Lègge per divertírsi, he reads to amuse himself.
Ho qualchecôsa da fáre, I have something to do.

c. "By" denoting the agent is *da*.

Ex.: *Fu fátto da lùi*, it was done by him.

d. "In" is *in;* but when expressing future time it is *fra*.

Ex.: *Fra tre giórni sarà finíto*, in three days it will be finished.

e. "For" is *per:* as *l' ha fátto per me*, "he has done it for me." But in the sense of "since," in speaking of past time, "for" is *da*. "For," meaning "during," is omitted or translated *duránte*. Sentences like "it is right for him to do it" must be translated by *che* with the subjunctive : *è giústo che lo fáccia*.

Ex.: *Dimóra da mólti ánni a Firènze*, he has lived for many years at Florence (see **73**).
Resterò cínque settimáne, I shall stay for five weeks.
Continuárono duránte tre sècoli, they continued for three centuries.
Pióvve duránte un mése, it rained for a month.
Bisógna ch' io váda, it is necessary for me to go.

f. "From" is *da;* but before adverbs and sometimes after verbs of departing it is *di.* In speaking of time it is generally *fin da.*

> Ex.: *È lontáno di qua,* it is far from here.
> *Èsco di cása,* I go out of the house.
> *Fin dal princípio,* from the beginning.

g. *Da* has, in addition to the meanings "by," "from," "since," another sense hard to render in English : it may be translated "as," "characteristic of," "destined for," "such as to," or "suited to," according to the context. *Da* means also "at the house of" or "to the house of." *Da* corresponds to English "on" or "at" before the word "side," *párte,* used in its literal sense.

> Ex.: *Prométto da uómo d' onóre,* I promise as a man of honor.
> *Il Salvíni da Otéllo,* Salvini as Othello.
> *Saréste tánto buóno da veníre,* would you be so good as to come?
> *Quésto è da sciôcchi,* this is acting like a fool.
> *Il bambíno ha un giudízio da gránde,* the child has the judgment of a grown person.
> *La sála da pránzo,* the dining-room.
> *Úna tázza da caffè,* a coffee-cup.
> *L' ho vedúto dal Signór Néri,* I saw him at Mr. Neri's.
> *Viéne da me,* he comes to my house.
> *Da quésta párte,* on this side.

h. *A* is often used before a noun — not indicating material (which is expressed by *di*) nor purpose (expressed by *da*) — that describes another noun, when in English these two substantives would form a compound word.

> Ex.: *Úna mácchina a vapóre,* a steam-engine.
> *Úna sédia a dóndolo,* a rocking-chair.
> *Úno sgabéllo a tre piédi,* a three-legged stool.

i. *Èssere per* or *stáre per* means "to be about to."

> Ex.: *Stáva per parláre,* he was on the point of speaking.

j. In some idiomatic phrases *di* is used in Italian when another preposition would be employed in English.

Ex.: *Di giórno, di nótte,* by day, by night.
Essere contènto di úna còsa, to be satisfied with a thing.
Vivo di páne. I live on bread.
Che facéva délle fòrbici, what did he do with the scissors?

ADVERBS.

80. (1) Adverbs, unless they begin the clause, are generally placed immediately after the verb; *non*, however, always precedes the verb. When a compound tense is used, the adverb nearly always follows the past participle, but *mái* and *sémpre* usually precede it. See also **84**.

Ex.: *Non ci vádo mái,* I never go there.
Ho parláto spésso, I have often spoken.
Non ha sémpre parláto così, he hasn't always talked so.

(2) Adverbs are compared like adjectives (see **31**); but "better," "worse," "more," "less" are respectively *méglio, péggio, più, méno.*

81. "Yes" is *sì* or *già:* *sì* when it expresses real affirmation, *già* when it denotes passive assent. "No" is *no.* "Not" is *non,* after which a word beginning with *s* impure generally prefixes *i.* "Or not" at the end of a clause is *o no.*

Ex.: *Le piáce quésto tèmpo? — Sì.* — "Do you like this weather?"
"Yes."
Che tempáccio! — Già. — "What nasty weather!" "Yes."
Sta bène, he is well; *non istà bène,* he isn't well.
Sia véro o no, whether it be true or not.

a. " What? " meaning " what do you say ? " is *cóme?* *Che* and the interjection *o* are often used to introduce questions.

Ex.: *O perchè non rispondète? — Cóme? — Che siète sórdo, signóre?* — " Why don't you answer? " " What? " "Are you deaf, sir? "

b. " Very " is *mólto* (see, however, 35, *a*). Instead of using a word or suffix for " very," the Italians often repeat the emphasized adjective or adverb.

Ex.: *È mólto béllo* or *è bellissimo*, it is very beautiful.
I suói genitóri èrano póveri póveri, his parents were very poor.

82. "Only " may be translated *soltánto* or *solaménte ;* but it is oftener rendered by *non . . . che*, with the whole verb intervening, and with the word modified by "only " immediately after *che*.

Ex.: *Non ne ho compráto che dúe*, I have bought only two of them.

83. "Never" is *non ... mái*, with the inflected part of the verb intervening. " Just," as an adverb of time, is *or óra*. " Early " is *présto, per témpo*, or *di buon' óra*. " This morning " is *stamáne ;* " last night " is *stanótte*. " The day after to-morrow " and " the day before yesterday " are respectively *domán l' áltro* and *ier l' áltro*. " A week, a fortnight from to-day " are *òggi a òtto, a quíndici*. " Ago " is translated by *fa*, which follows the substantive of time ; if this substantive is plural, " ago " may be rendered also by *sóno* (*èrano* or *saránno* if the date from which time is counted be past or future).

Ex.: *Non ti ha mái vedúto*, he has never seen thee.
Son arriváti or óra, they have just arrived.
Tre ánni fa, three years ago ; *quáttro giórni sóno*, four days ago.

Lunedì èrano dùe settimàne, two weeks ago Monday.
Domàni sarànno cìnque mèsi, five months ago to-morrow.

84. "Here" and "there" when they denote a place already mentioned, and no particular stress is laid upon them, are *ci* and *vi*, which occupy the same positions with respect to the verb as the pronouns *ci* and *vi* (see **48**; **49**, *a*) ; "there is," "there are," etc., are *c' è* or *vi è*, *ci sóno* or *vi sóno*, etc. *Ci* and *vi* are often used in Italian when they would be superfluous in English.

When emphasized, "here" is *qui* or *qua,* "there" indicating a place near the person addressed is *costì* or *costà,* and "there" denoting a point remote from both speaker and hearer is *lì* or *là.*

> Ex.: *Càrlo vi è tornàto,* Charles has gone back there.
> *Àlla scuòla non ci vàdo,* I don't go to school.
> *Vòi rimarrète costà, ègli resterà laggiù, ed lo non partirò di qui,* you will remain where you are, he will stay down there, and I shall not move from here.

a. "Here I am," "here it is," etc., are *èccomi, èccolo, èccola,* etc.

85. Most adverbs of manner are formed by adding *-ménte* to the feminine singular of the corresponding adjective. Adjectives in *-le* and *-re* drop their final *e* in forming the adverb.

> Ex.: *Fránco,* frank : *francaménte,* frankly.
> *Felìce,* happy ; *feliceménte,* happily.
> *Piacèvole,* pleasant : *piacevolménte,* pleasantly.
> *Piacevolìssimo,* very pleasant; *piacevolissimaménte,* very pleasantly.

a. "So" meaning "it" is translated *lo :* as *lo fàccio,* "I do so"; *lo créde,* "he thinks so"; *lo dìcono,* "they say so."

EXERCISE 19.

Agostíno è un golóso di prima ríga. Cóme[1] vedéva déi confêtti, úna chícca, délle frútta, súbito se le pigliáva e mangiáva sénza permésso, ánche se non êrano súe. Infíno i suôi compágni di scuôla lo rimproverávano di quésto viziáccio. La maêstra pensò di puníre Agostíno. Un giórno, quándo fu l' óra délla ricreazióne, tirò fuôri dálla súa cassétta de' confêtti, e mettêndoli nel paniêre d' Agostíno, gli dísse[2] : — Quésti li porterái a cása álla túa sorellína. — Agostíno a vedér que' confêtti féce[6] cêrti occhióni grôssi cóme quélli d' un bôve. Non istáva più in sè[3] dálla vôglia di mangiáre que' confêtti. Êra tánto golóso, che se avéva qualcôsa di súo non dáva núlla a nessúno ; êra tánto golóso, che avéva la sfacciatággine di mangiáre le côse dégli áltri ; o figurátevi dúnque cóme si struggéva di[4] mangiár que' confêtti ch' êrano nel súo panieríno. Finíta la refezióne, i bambíni vánno[5] nel giardíno. Appéna Agostíno véde che nélla stánza dov' êrano i panieríni non c' êra nessúno, sparísce dal giardíno, e vía a pigliáre i confêtti. Ma non ha finíto di buttár giù il prímo, che[1] sênte un amáro, un sapóre così cattívo da non potér rêggere ; spúta e rispúta, ma l' amáro non se ne andáva.[5] Êra curióso vedér Agostíno disperáto per quel saporáccio. E i compágni chi da un úscio, chi da un áltro, e chi dálla finêstra che dáva sul giardíno, stávano a vedérlo, e a rídere di quésta cêlia che la maêstra avéva fátto[6] a quel golóso. Allóra la maêstra gli dísse[2] : — Védi, Agostíno ; ho fátto[6] fáre quésti confêtti piêni d' assênzio appôsta per te ; védi a che côsa pôrta l' ingordígia ! Un áltro bambíno non ci sarêbbe rimásto a[7] quésta cêlia. — Agostíno si accôrse[8] che la signóra maêstra gli avéva fátta[6] quésta cêlia per súo bêne, e che se non si correggéva diventáva lo zimbêllo di tútti.

---

[1] When.   [2] *Dire.*   [3] He was beside himself.   [4] He was dying to.   [5] *Andáre, andársene.*   [6] *Fáre.*   [7] Wouldn't have been taken in by.   [8] *Accòrgersi.*

EXERCISE 20.

It is related that in by-gone[1] times a parrot escaped from a villa. This parrot had learned to say all-the-time[2]: "Who's-there[3]? who's-there[3]?" Having-fled[4] into a wood, it was flying from one tree to another without knowing where to go. A peasant, who by chance was hunting[5] in that place, eyed the parrot, and having never seen any birds before[6] of this sort, he was[7] amazed at-it,[8] and took[9] all-possible[10] care to aim straight with his gun, so-as-to shoot-it[11] and carry it to show off as a rare thing. But while the peasant was aiming, the parrot, seeing[4] him, repeated his usual question : "Who's-there[3]? who's-there[3]?" The-peasant's-blood-froze-in-his-veins[12] at those words ; and lowering[4] his gun, and taking-his-hat-from-his-head[13] he hastened to reply to him, dreadfully[14] mortified : "Excuse-me,[15] for-mercy's-sake,[16] I took[17] you for a bird ! "

[1] *Andàti.* [2] Always. [3] *Chi c' è.* [4] Past participle. [5] *A càccia.* [6] *Per l' innànzi.* [7] *Rimàse :* see **54,** *f.* [8] *Ne.* [9] Gave himself. [10] *Ogni.* [11] *Tiràrgli.* [12] To the peasant not remained blood in-him (*addòsso*). [13] *Levàtosi di càpo il cappèllo.* [14] *Tùtto.* [15] *La scùsi.* [16] For charity. [17] Had taken.

INDEFINITE PRONOUNS.

86. "**One**," "people," "we," "you," "they," used in an indefinite sense, are rendered in Italian by the reflexive construction with *si* (see **54,** *g*).

Ex.: *Si cànta bène in Itàlia*, they sing well in Italy.
Sì fa così, you do this way.
Si fànno spèsso quèste còse, one often does these things.

87. "**All**" as a substantive is *túlto* (*túlti*, etc.) : as *tacévano túlti*, "all were silent." The adjective "all," "the whole" is *túlto* followed by the definite article : as *túlta la têrra*, "the whole earth"; *túlto il giórno*, "all day"; *túlte le románe son bêlle*, "all Roman ladies are beautiful."

88. "**Any**," when it really adds nothing to the sense, is omitted : as *non ha líbri*, "he hasn't (any) books"; *voléte víno*, "do you want (any) wine?" When, however, this redundant "any" might be replaced by "any of the," it is translated by the partitive genitive (see **12**, *a*) : as *voléte del víno*, "do you want any (of the) wine?"

"Any" used substantively in the sense of "any of it," "any of them" is *ne* (see **47**, 3) : as *non ne ho*, "I haven't any"; *non ne ha più*, "he hasn't any more"; *ne avéte*, "have you any?"

"Any" meaning "any whatsoever" is *qualúnque:* as *lo fa mêglio di qualúnque áltra persóna*, "he does it better than any other person."

89. "**Some**," when it adds nothing to the sense, is omitted or rendered by the partitive genitive : as *voléte búrro* or *voléte del búrro*, "will you have some butter?"

"Some" meaning "some of it," "some of them" is *ne:* as *ne ha*, "he has some."

Otherwise "some" is *alcúno* or *quálche*. *Quálche* is always singular (even when the meaning is plural), and is never used substantively. Ex.: *alcúne persóne* or *quálche persóna*, "some persons"; *alcúni lo dícono*, "some say so."

90. "**Some . . . others**," "the one . . . the other," "one . . . another" are translated by *chi . . . chi, áltri . . . áltri, l' úno . . . l' áltro*, or *alcúni . . . alcúni*.

Alcúni used in this way is always plural. A verb whose subject is *chi* or *áltri* (used in this sense) is always singular ; *altri* is not used after prepositions. But *l' úno* and *l' áltro* can be used in any case or number.

> Ex.: *Tútti, chi più tósto, e chi méno, morívano,* all died, some sooner, some later.
> *Áltri cáde, áltri fúgge,* some fall, others flee.
> *Gli úni son buóni, gli áltri cattívi,* some are good, others bad.

91. Following is a list of some other indefinite pronouns and adjectives :—

Anybody, *qualcúno, qualchedúno, chicchessia,* pronouns.

Any more, *più, ne . . . più,* pron.

Anything, *qualchecósa,* pron.

Anything else, *áltro,* pron.

Both, *tútti e dúe, l' úno e l' áltro, ambedúe,* pron. or adj.

Certain, *cérto,* adj.

Each, *ógni, ciascúno, ognúno,* adj.

Either, *l' úno o l' áltro,* pron. or adj.

Every, *ógni, ciascúno, ognúno, ciaschedúno,* adj.

Everybody, *tútti* (pl.), *ciaschedúno, ciascúno, ognúno,* pron.

Everything, *tútto,* pron.

Few, a few, *póchi* (pl.), pron. or adj.

However much, (or many), *per quanto* (*-ti*), adj.

Little, *póco,* pron. or adj.

Less, *méno,* pron. or adj.*

Many, *mólti,* pron. or adj.†

More, *più,* pron. or adj.

Much, *mólto,* pron. or adj.

Neither, *non . . . l' úno nè l' áltro, nè l' úno nè l' áltro,* pron. or adj.

No, *non . . . nessúno, non . . . alcúno,* adj.

Nobody, *non . . . nessúno,* pron.

No more, *non ne . . . più,* pron., *non . . . più,* adj.

None, *non ne . . .,* pron.

Nothing, *non . . . niénte, non . . . núlla,* pron.

Nothing else, *non . . . più niénte, non . . . più núlla,* pron.

Others, *altrúi* (see **91**, *d*), pron.

Several, *parécchi* (fem. *parécchie*), pron. or adj.

Somebody, *qualchedúno, qualcúno,* pron.

Something, *qualchecósa,* pron.

Such, *tále,* adj.

Such a, *un tále,* adj. (but also pron. in Ital., meaning "so-and-so").

Whatever, *qualúnque* (invariable), adj.

---

* "Less " = "smaller " is *più piccolo.*   † ".A great many " is *moltissimi.*

a. The verb used with *nessúno*, *alcúno*, *niénte*, *núlla* (meaning "no," "nobody," "nothing") must be preceded by *non*, "not," unless the pronoun precedes the verb.

Ex.: *Non ho vísto nessúno*, I have seen nobody.
Nessún pópolo lo possiéde, no people possesses it.

b. "Nothing" followed by an adjective is *niénte di*.

Ex.: *Non avéte niénte di buôno*, you have nothing good.

c. *Ciascúno*, *ciaschedúno*, *ognúno*, *nessúno*, and *alcúno* when used adjectively are inflected like *úno* (see **14**, **15**).

d. *Altrúi*, "another," "others," "our neighbor," is invariable, and is not used as subject of a verb: as *con altrúi*, "with other people"; *chi áma altrúi áma sè stésso*, "he who loves his neighbor loves himself." The prepositions *di* and *a* are sometimes omitted before it: as *la móstro altrúi*, "I point her out to others"; *la vóglia altrúi*, "the will of another."

EXERCISE 21.

Per mutáre[1]! Riccárdo dice[2] mále di qualchedúno. Che brútto vízio è mái quéllo! A sentír Riccárdo, tútti son ásini, tútti sóno cattívi; di buôni e di brávi non c'è che lúi. Ma oramái ognúno ha conosciúto di che pánni véste,[3] e nessúno gli créde più. Se fósse brávo e buôno, si guarderêbbe dal dir mále di quésto e di quéllo, ánche quándo ne avésse quálche ragióne. Figurátevi, dúnque, se può[4] éssere buôno e brávo lúi che dice mále di tútti! Sôrte, ripêto, che nessúno gli créde più, e quándo si sênte dir mále di qualchedúno, e si sa[5] che c'è Riccárdo di mêzzo,[6] ognúno si affrétta a rispóndere: Se l' ha détto[2] quel maldicênte di Riccárdo, non è véro núlla dicêrto.

---

[1] There he is at it again! [2] *Díre*. [3] What sort of a fellow he is. [4] *Potére*. [5] *Sapére*. [6] At the bottom of it.

LIST OF IRREGULAR VERBS ARRANGED ACCORDING TO CONJUGATION.*

92. This list contains no compound verbs except those which differ in conjugation from their simple verbs and those for which no simple verb exists in Italian. It does not include a few irregular defective verbs † seldom or never used in modern Italian, which are .to be found in the Alphabetical List of Irregular and Defective Verbs beginning on page 100.

With every verb its irregular forms are given : in the same line with the infinitive are the present participle (if it be needed to show the original form of the infinitive), the first person singular of the preterite indicative, the past participle, and the first person singular of the future indicative (if the future be contracted) : immediately below are the present indicative, the imperative, and the present subjunctive, if these parts be peculiar.

All tenses not mentioned are regular. Preterites in *-ái*, *-éi*, *-ii* are regular throughout.

FIRST CONJUGATION.

1. Andáre, *to go*, andái, andáto ; andrò.

PRES. IND.		IMPER.		PRES. SUBJ.	
Vádo *or* vo,	andiámo,	Va',		Váda,	andiámo,
vái,	andáte,	andáte.		váda,	andiáte,
va,	vánno.			váda,	vádano.

---

2. Fáre, *to do*, facêndo, féci, fátto ; farò.

PRES. IND.	IMPER.	PRES. SUBJ.
Fáccio *or* fo, facciámo,	Fa',	Fáccia, facciámo,
fái, fáte,	fáte.	fáccia, facciáte,
fa, fánno.		fáccia, fácciano.

3. Dáre, *to give*, diêdi, dáto ; darò. *Imp. subj.* déssi.

PRES. IND.	PRET. IND.	IMPER.	PRES. SUBJ.
Do,	Diêdi (*or* détti),		Día,
dái,	désti,	Da',	día,
dà,	diêde (*or* détte),		día,
diámo,	démmo,		diámo,
dáte,	déste,	dáte.	diáte,
dánno.	diêdero (*or* déttero).		díano *or* díeno.

4. Stáre (68, *a*), *to stand*, stétti, státo ; starò. *Imp. subj.* stéssi.

PRES. IND.	PRET. IND.	IMPER.	PRES. SUBJ.
Sto,	Stétti,		Stía,
stái,	stésti,	Sta',	stía,
sta,	stétte,		stía,
stiámo,	stémmo,		stiámo,
státe,	stéste,	státe.	stiáte,
stánno.	stéttero.		stíano *or* stíeno.

SECOND CONJUGATION.

5. Avére, *to have*, êbbi, avúto ; avrò. See **53**, *b*.

6. Sapére, *to know*, sêppi, sapúto ; saprò.

PRES. IND.	IMPER.	PRES. SUBJ.
So, sappiámo,	Sáppi,	Sáppia, sappiámo,
sái, sapéte,	sappiáte.	sáppia, sappiáte,
sa, sánno.		sáppia, sáppiano.

7. Cadére, *to fall*, cáddi, cadúto ; cadrò *or* caderò.

PRES. IND.		PRES. SUBJ.	
Cádo (cággio),	cadiámo (caggiámo),	Cáda (cággia),	cadiámo (caggiámo),
cádi,	cadéte,	cáda (cággia),	cadiáte,
cáde,	cádono (cággiono).	cáda (cággia),	cádano (cággiano).

8. Dovére, *to owe*, dovéi (*or* dovétti), dovúto ; dovrò. *Imper. lacking.*

PRES. IND.	PRES. SUBJ.
Dèvo *or* dèbbo (*or* dèggio),	Dèbba (dèggia),
dèvi,	dèbba (dèggia),
dève *or* dèbbe,	dèbba (dèggia),
dobbiámo (deggiámo)	dobbiámo,
dovéte,	dobbiáte,
dèvono *or* dèbbono (*or* dèggiono).*	dèbbano (dèggiano).

9. Sedére, *to sit*, sedéi *or* sedétti, sedúto.

PRES. IND.		PRES. SUBJ.	
Sièdo *or* sèggo,	sediámo *or* seggiámo,	Sièda *or* sègga,	sediámo *or* seggiámo,
sièdi,	sedéte,	sièda *or* sègga,	sediáte,
siède,	sièdono *or* sèggono.	sièda *or* sègga,	sièdano *or* sèggano.

10. Vedére, *to see*, vídi, vedúto *or* vísto ; vedrò.†

PRES. IND.	PRES. SUBJ.
Védo (véggo *or* véggio),	Véda (végga *or* véggia),
védi,	véda (végga *or* véggia),
véde,	véda (végga *or* véggia),
vediámo (veggiámo),	vediámo (veggiámo),
vedéte,	vediáte (veggiáte),
védono (véggono *or* véggiono).	védano (véggano *or* véggiano).

11. Giacére, *to lie*, giácqui, giaciúto.

PRES. IND.		PRES. SUBJ.	
Giáccio,	giacciámo,	Giáccia,	giacciámo,
giáci,	giacéte,	giáccia,	giacciáte,
giáce,	giácciono.	giáccia,	giácciano.

12. Piacére, *to please: like* giacére (11).
13. Tacére, *to be silent: like* giacére (11).
14. Solére, *to be wont*, sólito. *Pret., fut., cond., and imper. lacking.*

---

* Also dènno, dènno.　† Provvedére : provvederò.

PRES. IND.		PRES. SUBJ.	
Sôglio,	sogliámo,	Sôglia,	sogliámo,
suôli,	soléte,	sôglia,	sogliáte,
suôle,	sôgliono.	sôglia,	sôgliano.

15. Dolére, *to grieve*, dôlsi, dolúto ; dorrò.

PRES. IND		PRES. SUBJ.	
Dôlgo *or* dôglio,	dogliámo,	Dôlga *or* dôglia,	dogliámo,
duôli,	doléte,	dôlga *or* dôglia,	dogliáte,
duôle,	dôlgono *or* dôgliono.	dôlga *or* dôglia,	dôlgano *or* dôgliano.

16. Rimanére, *to remain*, rimási, rimásto *or* rimáso ; rimarrò.

PRES. IND.		PRES. SUBJ.	
Rimángo,	rimaniámo,	Rimánga,	rimaniámo,
rimáni,	rimanéte,	rimánga,	rimaniáte,
rimáne,	rimángono.	rimánga,	rimángano.

17. Tenére, *to hold*, ténni, tenúto ; terrò.

PRES. IND.		PRES. SUBJ.	
Têngo,	teniámo,	Tênga,	teniámo,
tiêni,	tenéte,	tênga,	teniáte,
tiêne,	têngono.	tênga,	têngano.

18. Valére, *to be worth*, válsi, valúto *or* válso ; varrò.

PRES. IND.		PRES. SUBJ.	
Válgo *or* váglio,	vagliámo,	Válga *or* váglia,	vagliámo,
váli,	valéte,	válga *or* váglia,	vagliáte,
vále,	válgono *or* vágliono.	válga *or* váglia,	válgano *or* vágliano.

19. Volére, *to wish*, vôlli, volúto ; vorrò.

PRES. IND.		IMPER.	PRES. SUBJ.	
Vôglio,	vogliámo,	Vôgli,	Vôglia,	vogliámo,
vuôi,	voléte,	vogliáte.	vôglia,	vogliáte,
vuôle,	vôgliono.		vôglia,	vôgliano.

20. Paróre, *to seem*, párvi, parúto *or* párso ; parrò.

PRES. IND.		PRES. SUBJ.	
Páio,	pariámo *or* paiámo,	Páia,	pariámo *or* paiámo,
pári,	paréte,	páia,	paiáte,
páre,	páiono.	páia,	páiano.

21. Potére, *to be able*, potéi, potúto ; potrò. *Imper. lacking.*

PRES. IND.		PRES. SUBJ.	
Pôsso,	possiámo,	Pôssa,	possiámo,
puôi, .	potéte,	pôssa,	possiáte,
può,	pôssono.	pôssa,	pôssano.

22. Persuadére, *to persuade*, persuási, persuáso.
23. Calére, *to matter*, cálse, calúto. *Impersonal. Fut., cond., and imper. lacking.*

PRES. IND.	PRES. SUBJ.
Cále.	Cáglia.

THIRD CONJUGATION.

FIRST CLASS : -si, -so.

24. Accêndere, *to light*, accési, accéso.
25. Allúdere, *to allude*, allúsi (alludéi), allúso.
26. Árdere, *to burn*, ársi, árso.
27. Assídere, *to besiege*, assísi, assíso.
28. Chiúdere, *to shut*, chiúsi, chiúso.
29. Conquídere, *to conquer*, conquísi, conquíso.
30. Contúndere, *to bruise*, contúsi, contúso.
31. Córrere, *to run*, córsi, córso.
32. Decídere, *to decide*, decísi, decíso.
33. Difêndere, *to defend*, difési (difendéi), diféso (difendúto).
34. Divídere, *to divide*, divísi, divíso.
35. Elídere, *to elide*, elísi, elíso.

36. Elúdere, *to elude*, elúsi (eludéi *or* eludétti), elúso.
37. Esplôdere, *to explode*, esplôsi, esplôso.
38. Intrídere, *to dilute*, intrísi, intríso.
39. Intrúdere, *to intrude*, intrúsi, intrúso.
40. Invádere, *to invade*, invási, inváso.
41. Lêdere, *to offend*, lêsi, lêso.
42. Lúdere, *to play*, lúsi, lúso.
43. Mêrgere, *to plunge*, mêrsi, mêrso.
44. Môrdere, *to bite*, môrsi, môrso.
45. Offêndere, *to offend*, offési, offéso.
46. Pêrdere, *to lose*, perdéi *or* pêrsi, perdúto *or* pêrso.
47. Prêndere, *to take*, prési (prendéi), préso.
48. Rádere, *to shave*, rási (radéi), ráso.
49. Rêndere, *to render*, rési (rendéi), réso (rendúto).
50. Rídere, *to laugh*, rísi, ríso.
51. Rifúlgere, *to shine*, rifúlsi, rifúlso.
52. Ródere, *to gnaw*, rósi, róso.
53. Scéndere, *to descend*, scési, scéso.
54. Scêrnere, *to discern*, scernéi *or* scêrsi, scernúto *or* scêrso.
55. Sospêndere, *to suspend*, sospési, sospéso.
56. Spárgere, *to scatter*, spársi, spárso.
57. Spêndere, *to spend*, spési, spéso.
58. Spêrgere, *to disperse*, spêrsi, spêrso.
59. Têndere (*trans.*), *to extend*, tési, téso.
60. Têrgere, *to wipe*, têrsi, têrso.
61. Uccídere, *to kill*, uccísi, uccíso.

MORE IRREGULAR.

62. Espêllere, *to expel*, espúlsi, espúlso.
63. Fóndere, *to melt*, fúsi (fondéi), fúso (fondúto).
64. Chiêdere, *to ask*, chiési, chiêsto.
65. Nascóndere, *to hide*, nascósi, nascósto.
66. Pórre, *to put*, ponêndo, pósi, pósto; porrò.

PRES. IND.		PRES. SUBJ.	
Póngo,	poniámo (ponghiámo),	Pónga,	poniámo (ponghiámo),
póni,	ponéte.	pónga,	poniáte,
póne,	póngono.	pónga,	póngano.

67. Rispóndere, *to answer*, rispósi, rispósto.

SECOND CLASS: -si, -to.

68. Assôrbere, *to absorb*, assôrsi, assôrto.
69. Distínguere, *to distinguish*, distínsi, distínto.
70. Êrgere, *to erect*, êrsi, êrto.
71. Fíngere, *to feign*, fínsi, fínto.
72. Frángere, *to break*, fránsi, fránto.
73. Consúmere, *to consume*, consúnsi, consúnto.
74. Pôrgere, *to present*, pôrsi, pôrto.
75. Redímere, *to redeem*, redênsi (rediméi), redênto.
76. Scíndere, *to sever*, scindéi *or* scínsi, scindúto *or* scínto.
77. Scôrgere, *to perceive*, scôrsi, scôrto.
78. Sórgere, *to rise*, sórsi, sórto.
79. Spándere, *to spill*, spánsi, spánto.
80. Spôrgere, *to project*, spôrsi, spôrto.
81. Tôrcere, *to twist*, tôrsi, tôrto.
82. Víncere, *to conquer*, vínsi, vínto.
83. Vôlgere, *to turn*, vôlsi, vôlto.

More Irregular.

84. Assôlvere, *to absolve*, assôlsi (assolvétti), assôlto *or* assolúto.
85. Côgliere (côrre), *to gather*, côlsi, cúlto ; coglierò *or* corrò.

PRES. IND.		PRES. SUBJ.	
Côlgo,	cogliámo,	Côlga,	cogliámo,
côgli,	cogliéte,	côlga,	cogliáte,
côglie,	côlgono.	côlga,	côlgano.

86. Scégliere (scérre), *to choose: like* côgliere (85).
87. Sciôgliere (sciôrre), *to untie: like* côgliere (85).

88. Tôgliere (tôrre), *to take: like* côgliere (85).
89. Giúngere (giúgnere), *to arrive,* giúnsi, giúnto ; giungerò (giugnerò).

PRES. IND.	PRES. SUBJ.
Giúngo *or* giúgno,	Giúnga *or* giúgna,
giúngi *or* giúgni,	giúnga *or* giúgna,
giúnge *or* giúgne,	giúnga *or* giúgna,
giungiámo *or* giugniámo,	giungiámo *or* giugniámo,
giungéte *or* giugnéte,	giungiáte *or* giugniáte,
giúngono *or* giúgnono.	giúngano *or* giúgnano.

90. Cíngere (cígnere), *to gird: like* giúngere (89).
91. Múngere (múgnere), *to milk: like* giúngere (89).
92. Piángere (piágnere), *to weep: like* giúngere (89).
93. Píngere (pígnere), *to paint: like* giúngere (89).
94. Púngere (púgnere), *to prick: like* giúngere (89).
95. Spêgnere (spêngere), *to extinguish: like* giúngere (89), *except that the forms with* gn *are the usual ones throughout.*
96. Spíngere (spígnere), *to push: like* giúngere (89).
97. Stríngere (strígnere), *to bind: like* giúngere (89).
98. Tíngere (tignere), *to dye: like* giúngere (89).
99. Úngere (úgnere), *to anoint: like* giúngere (89).
100. Vêllere (vêrre), *to tear up,* vêlsi, vêlto.

PRES. IND.		PRES. SUBJ.	
Vêllo *or* vêlgo,	velliámo,	Vêlla *or* vêlga,	velliámo,
vêlli,	velléte,	vêlla *or* vêlga,	velliáte,
vêlle,	vêllono *or* vêlgono.	vêlla *or* vêlga,	vêllano *or* vêlgano

THIRD CLASS : -ssi, -sso.

101. Connêttere, *to connect,* connêssi (connettéi), connêsso (connettúto).
102. Genuflêttere, *to kneel,* genuflêssi, genuflêsso.

103. Riflêttere, *to reflect,** riflettéi *or* riflêssi, riflettúto *or* riflêsso.
104. Méttere, *to put*, méssi *or* mísi, mésso.
105. Discútere, *to discuss*, discússi, discússo.
106. Esprimere, *to express*, esprêssi, esprêsso.
107. Fêndere, *to split*, fendéi (fendétti *or* fêssi), fendúto *or* fêsso.
108. Fíggere (fígere), *to fix*, físsi (físi), físso (físo) *or* fítto.
109. Rilúcere, *to shine*, rilússi *or* rilucéi. *Past part. lacking.*
110. Succêdere, *to happen*, succêssi *or* succedéi, succêsso *or* succedúto.
111. Muôvere, *to move*, movêndo, môssi, môsso.
112. Scuôtere, *to shake*, scotêndo, scôssi, scôsso.

FOURTH CLASS: -ssi, -tto.

113. Afflíggere, *to afflict*, afflíssi, afflítto.
114. Cuôcere, *to cook*, cocêndo, côssi, côtto.
115. Dirígere, *to direct*, dirêssi, dirêtto.
116. Fríggere, *to fry*, fríssi, frítto.
117. Lêggere, *to read*, lêssi, lêtto.
118. Negligere, *to neglect*, neglêssi, neglêtto.
119. Protêggere, *to protect*, protêssi, protêtto.
120. Rêggere, *to support*, rêssi, rêtto.
121. Scrívere, *to write*, scríssi, scrítto.
122. Strúggere, *to melt*, strússi, strútto.

MORE IRREGULAR.

123. Condúrre, *to conduct*, conducêndo, condússi, condótto; condurrò.

PRES. IND.		PRES. SUBJ.	
Condúco,	conduciámo,	Condúca,	conduciámo,
condúci,	conducéte,	condúca,	conduciáte,
condúce,	condúcono.	condúca,	condúcano.

---

* When *riflêttere* means "to reflect light" it is irregular; when it means "to meditate" it is regular.

124. Trárre (tráere), *to drag*, traêndo, trássi, trátto ; trarrò.

PRES. IND.		PRES. SUBJ.	
Tràggo,	traiámo *or* traggiámo,	Trágga,	traiámo *or* traggiámo,
trái (tràggi),	tracte,	trágga,	traiáte,
tráe (trágge),	trággono.	trágga,	tràggano.

NOT CLASSIFIED.

125. Bére *or* bévere, *to drink*, bevêndo, bévvi (bevétti), bevúto ; berò *or* beverò.

PRES. IND.		PRES. SUBJ.	
Bévo *or* béo,	beviámo *or* beiámo,	Béva *or* béa,	beviámo *or* beiámo,
bévi *or* béi,	bevéte *or* beéte,	béva *or* béa,	beviáte *or* beiáte,
béve *or* bée,	bévono *or* béono.	béva *or* béa,	bévano *or* béano.

126. Conóscere, *to know*, conóbbi, conosciúto.

127. Créscere, *to grow*, crébbi, cresciúto.

128. Náscere, *to be born*, nácqui, náto.

129. Nuôcere, *to harm*, nocêndo, nôcqui, nociúto.

130. Esígere, *to exact*, esigéi, esátto.

131. Esístere, *to exist*, esistéi, esistíto.

132. Êssere, *to be*, fúi, státo ; sarò. See 53, *a* (and 67, *b*).

133. Piôvere, *to rain*, piôvve (piovè), piovúto. *Impersonal.*

134. Rómpere, *to break*, rúppi, rótto.

135. Sôlvere, *to undo*, solvéi (solvétti), solúto.

136. Vívere, *to live*, víssi, vissúto *or* vivúto.

FOURTH CONJUGATION.

137. Apríre, *to open*, apríi *or* apêrsi, apêrto.*

138. Coprire (cuoprire), *to cover: like* aprire (137).*

139. Offrire (offerire), *to offer*, offríi (offeríi) *or* offêrsi, offêrto.*

140. Soffrire (sofferire), *to suffer: like* offrire (139).*

141. Convertire, *to convert*, convertíi *or* convêrsi, convertíto *or* convêrso.*

---

* Present after the model of *sentire*, p. 59.

142. Costruíre (construíre), *to construct*, co(n)strússi *or* co(n)-
struíi, co(n)struíto *or* co(n)strútto.*
143. Digerire, *to digest*, digeríi, digeríto *or* digêsto.*
144. Esauríre, *to exhaust*, esauríi, esauríto *or* esáusto.*
145. Seppellíre, *to bury*, seppellíi, seppellíto *or* sepólto.*
146. Seguíre, *to follow*, seguíi, seguíto.

PRES. IND.		PRES. SUBJ.	
Sêguo (siêguo),	seguiámo,	Sêgua (siêgua),	seguiámo,
sêgui (siêgui),	seguíte,	. sêgua (siêgua),	seguiáte,
sêgue (siêgue),	sêguono (siêguono).	sêgua (siêgua),	sêguano (siêguano).

147. Cucíre, *to sew*, cucíi, cucíto.

PRES. IND.		PRES. SUBJ.	
Cúcio,	cuciámo,	Cúcia,	cuciámo,
cúci,	cucíte,	cúcia,	cuciáte,
cúce,	cúciono.	cúcia,	cúciano.

148. Sdrucíre *or* sdruscíre, *to rip: like* cucíre (147).
149. Empíre *or* émpiere, *to fill*, empiêndo, empíi, empíto. *All
but the present from the stem of* empíre.

PRES. IND.		PRES. SUBJ.	
Êmpio (empísco),	empiámo,	Émpia,	empiámo,
émpi (empísci),	empíte,	émpia,	empiáte,
émpie (empísce),	émpiono (empíscono).	émpia,	émpiano.

150. Moríre, *to die*, moríi, môrto; morirò *or* morrò.

PRES. IND.	PRES. SUBJ.
Muôio (muôro),.	muôia *or* muôra,
muôri,	muôia *or* muôra,
muôre,	muôia *or* muôra,
moriámo *or* muoiámo,	moriámo *or* muoiámo,
moríte,	muoiáte,
muôiono (muôrono).	muôiano *or* muôrano.

151. Sparíre, *to disappear*, sparíi *or* spárvi, sparíto.

---

* Present after the model of *finíre*, p. 58.

PRES. IND.	PRES. SUBJ.
Sparísco (spáio),	Sparísca (spáia),
sparísci,	sparísca (spáia),
sparísce,	sparísca (spáia),
spariámo,	spariámo,
sparíte,	spariáte,
sparíscono (spáiono).	sparíscano (spáiano).

152. Díre, *to say*, dicêndo, díssi, détto ; dirò.

PRES. IND.		IMPER.	PRES. SUBJ.	
Díco,	diciámo,	Di,	Díca,	diciámo,
díci,	díte,	díte.	díca,	diciáte,
díce,	dícono.		díca,	dícano.

153. Salíre, *to ascend*, salíi *or* sálsi, salíto.

PRES. IND.		PRES. SUBJ.	
Sálgo (salísco),	saliámo *or* sagliámo,	Sálga (salísca),	saliámo *or* sagliámo,
sáli (salísci),	salíte,	sálga (salísca),	sagliáte,
sále (salísce),	sálgono (salíscono).	sálga (salísca),	sálgano (salíscano).

154. Veníre, *to come*, vénni, venúto ; verrò.

PRES. IND.		PRES. SUBJ.	
Vêngo,	veniámo,	Vênga,	veniámo,
viêni,	veníte,	vênga,	veniáte,
viêne,	vêngono.	vênga,	vêngano.

155. Udíre, *to hear*, udíi, udíto.

PRES. IND.		PRES. SUBJ.	
Ôdo,	udiámo,	Ôda,	udiámo,
ôdi,	udíte,	ôda,	udiáte,
ôde,	ôdono.	ôda,	ôdano.

156. Uscíre (escíre), *to go out*, uscíi, uscíto.

PRES. IND.		PRES. SUBJ.	
Êsco,	usciámo,	Êsca,	usciámo,
êsci,	uscíte,	êsca,	usciáte,
êsce,	êscono.	êsca,	êscano.

ALPHABETICAL LIST OF IRREGULAR AND DEFECTIVE VERBS.

93. Following is a list of the Italian irregular and defective verbs. With every defective verb is a list of its existing forms. Every irregular verb is followed by a number referring to the list beginning on page 88. Compound verbs have, in general, been excluded from this list, unless they differ in conjugation from the simple verbs from which they come (see **68**, *a*). The commonest prefixes are: *a-* (corresponding to the preposition *a*), after which the simple verb doubles its initial consonant; *as-* (= Latin *abs*); *com-, con-, co-, cor-* (= prep. *con*); *de-, di-* (= prep. *di*); *dis-* (= Lat. *dis-*); *e-, es-* (= Lat. *ex*); *im-, in-* (= prep. *in*); *o-* (= Lat. *ob*), after which the verb generally doubles its initial consonant; *per* (= prep. *per*); *pre-* (= Lat. *prе-* or *prac-*); *pro-* (= Lat. *pro-*); *r-, re-, ri-* (= Lat. *re-*); *s-* (= Lat. *ex-* or *dis-*); *so-* or *su-* (= Lat. *sub*), after which the verb generally doubles its initial consonant; *sopra-, sopr-* (= prep. *sópra*); *sor-* (= prep. *su*); *sos-* (= Lat. *sub*); *sotto-, sott-* (= prep. *sótto*); *tra-* (= prep. *tra*).

Accadére, *see* cadére, 7.

Accêndere, 24.

Accôrgere, *see* scôrgere, 77.

Acquisire (*defect.*) : acquisíto.

Addúrre, *see* condúrre, 123.

Afflíggere, 113.

Álgere (*defect.*) : *Pret.* álsi, etc.

Allúdere, 25.

Ancídere, *see* uccídere, 61.

Andáre, 1.

Ángere (*defect.*) : *Pres.* ánge, ángono.

Annêttere, *see* connêttere, 101.

Antivedére, *Past Part. only* antivedúto, *otherwise like* vedére, 10.

Apparíre, *see* sparíre, 151.

Appêndere, *see* sospêndere, 55.

Apríre, 137.

Árdere, 26.

Arrôgere (*defect.*) : arrogêndo; arrôso *or* arrôto; *Pres.* arrôge; *Imp.* arrogéva; *Pret.* arrôse, arrôsero.

Ascéndere, *see* scéndere, 53.

Ascóndere, *see* nascóndere, 65.

Assídere, 27.

Assístere, *see* esístere, 131.

Assôlvere, 84.

Assôrbere, 68.

Assúmere, *see* consúmere, 73.

Avére, 5.

Bére, 125.

Bévere, *see* bére, 125.

Cadére, 7.

Calére, 23.

Cápere (*defect.*) : *Pres.* cápe; *Imp.* capéva.

Cèdere, *generally regular, sometimes has a Pret.* cêssi.

Chèrere (*defect.*) : *Pres.* chêro, chêre.

Chièdere, 64.

Chiúdere, 28.

Cíngere, 90.

Circoncídere, *see* decídere, 32.

Côgliere, 85.

Côlere (*defect.*) . colêndo, cólto; *Pres.* côlo, côle.

Comparíre, *see* sparíre, 151.

Comprímere, *see* esprímere, 106.

Concêdere, *see* succêdere, 110.

Concútere, *see* discútere, 105.

Condúrre, 123.

Connêttere, 101.

Conóscere, 126.

Conquídere, 29.

Consístere, *see* esístere, 131.

Constáre *is reg.*

Construíre, 142.

Consúmere, 73.

Contrastáre *is reg.*

Controvêrtere (*defect.*) : *Pres. and Imp. regular.*

Contúndere, 30.

Convêrgere, *reg. verb, has no Past Part.*

Convertíre, 141.

Copríre, 138.

Côrre, *see* côgliere, 85.

Córrere, 31.

Corrispóndere, *see* rispóndere, 67.

Costruíre, 142.

Créscere, 127.

Cuôcere, 114.

Cucíre, 147.

Dáre, 3.

Decídere, 32.

Dedúrre, *see* condúrre, 123.

Delínquere, *reg. verb, has no Past Part., and its Pret. (which is de-linquétti) is rare.*

Deprímere, *see* esprímere, 106.

Desístere, *see* esístere, 131.

Difêndere, 33.

Digeríre, 143.

Díre, 152.

Dirígere, 115.

Discéndere, *see* scéndere, 53.

Discútere, 105.

Dissôlvere, *see* sôlvere, 135.

Dissuadére, *see* persuadére, 22.

Distáre, *reg. in Pres. of all moods, Pres. Part. lacking, otherwise like* stáre, 4.

Distínguere, 69.

Distrúggere, *see* strúggere, 122.

Divedére (*defect.*) : *only Infin. used.*

Divídere, 34.

Dolére, 15.

Dovére, 8.

Elêggere, *see* lêggere, 117.

Elídere, 35.

Elúdere, 36.

Émpiere, *see* empíre, 149.

Empíre, 149.

Êrgere, 70.

Erígere, *see* dirígere, 115.

Esauríre, 144.

Escíre, *see* uscíre, 156.

Esclúdere, *see* chiúdere, 28.

Esígere, 130.

Esístere, 131.

Espêllere, 62.

Esplôdere, 37.

Esprímere, 106.

Êssere, 132.

Estínguere, *see* distínguere, 69.

Estôllere (*defect.*): *Pret. and Past Part. lacking; rest regular.*

Fáre, 2.

Fêndere, 107.

Fiêdere (*defect.*): *Pres.* fiêdo, fiêdi, fiêde, fiêdono; *Fut., Cond., Imper., and Past Part. lacking; rest regular.*

Fíggere, 108.

Fíngere, 71.

Folcíre (*defect.*): *Pres.* fólce; *Imp. Subj.* folcísse.

Fóndere, 63.

Frángere, 72.

Fríggere, 116.

Fúngere (*defect.*): *Pres., Imp., and Fut. regular.*

Genuflêttere, 102.

Giacére, 11.

Gíre (*defect.*): *Pres.* gíte; *Imper.,* gíte; *Pres. Subj.,* giámo, giáte; *Pres. Part. lacking; rest regular.*

Giúngere, 89.

Illúdere, *see* lúdere, 42.

Impêllere, *see* espêllere, 62.

Imprímere, *see* esprímere, 106.

Incídere, *see* decídere, 32.

Incútere, *see* discútere, 105.

Indúrre, *see* condúrre, 123.

Insístere, *see* esístere, 131.

Instáre *is reg.*

Instruíre, *see* construíre, 142.

Intercêdere, *see* succêdere, 110.

Intrídere, 38.

Introdúrre, *see* condúrre, 123.

Intrúdere, 39.

Inváderc, 40.

Invalére, *Past Part. only* inválso, *otherwise like* valére, 18.

Íre (*defect.*): *Pres.* íte ; *Imp. regular ; Pret.* ísti, íste ; *Fut.* irémo, iréte, iránno; *Imper.* íte; *Imp. Subj.* ísse, íste, íssero; *Past Part.* íto.

Istruíre, *see* costruíre, 142.

Lécere, *see* lícere.

Lêdere, 41.

Lêggere, 117.

Lícere (*defect.*): *Pres.* líce *or* léce ; *Past part.* lícito *or* lécito.

Lúcere (*defect.*): *Past Part. lacking, also first pers. sing. of Indic. Pres. and Pret.; rest regular.*

Lúdere, 42.

Mantenére, *see* tenére, 17.

Mêrgere, 43.

Méttere, 104.

Môlcere (*defect.*): *Pres.* môlce; *Imp.* molcéva.

Môrdere, 44.

Moríre, 150.

Muôvere, 111.

Múngere, 91.

Náscere, 128.

Nascóndere, 65.

Neglígere, 118.

Nuôcere, 129.

Offêndere, 45.

Offeríre, *see* offríre, 139.

Offríre, 139.

Olíre (*defect.*) : *Imp.* olíva, olívi, olíva, olívano.

Opprímere, *see* esprímere, 106.

Ostáre *is reg.*

Parére, 20.

Páve (*defect., Infin. not found*).

Percípere (*defect.*): *Pres., Imp., and Fut. regular ; Past Part.* percétto.

Percuôtere, *see* scuôtere, 112.

Pêrdere, 46.

Permanére, *see* rimanére, 16.

Persístere, *see* esístere, 131.

Persuadére, 22.

Piacére, 12.

Piángere, 92.

Píngere, 93.

Piôvere, 133.

Pôrgere, 74.

Pórre, 66.

Possedére, *see* sedére, 9.

Potére, 21.

Precídere, *see* decídere, 32.

Prêndere, 47.

Presúmere, *see* consúmere, 73.

Prodúrre, *see* condúrre, 123.

Protêggere, 119.

Provvedére, *Fut. and Cond. uncontracted, otherwise like* vedére, 10.

Prúdere, *reg. verb, has no Past Part., and first and second persons are rare throughout.*

Púngere, 94.

Raccôgliere, *see* côgliere, 85.

Rádere, 48.

Raggiúngere, *see* giúngere, 89.

Rêcere (*defect.*) : *Pres.* rêce, rêciono.

Recídere, *see* decídere, 32.

Redímere, 75.

Rêggere, 120.

Rêndere, 49.

Repêllere, *see* espêllere, 62.

Reprímere, *see* esprímere, 106.

Resístere, *see* esístere, 131.

Restáre *is reg.*

Rídere, 50.

Ridúrre, *see* condúrre, 123.

Riêdere (*defect.*): *Pres.* riêdo, riêdi, riêde, riêdono; *Imp.* redíva; *Pret.* redí, redírono; *Pres. Subj.* riêda, riêdano; *Imp. Subj.* riedísse.

Riflêttere, 103.

Rifúlgere, 51.

Rilúcere, 109.

Rimanére, 16.

Risôlvere (*to dissolve*), *see* sôlvere, 135.

Risôlvere (*to determine*), *see* assôlvere, 84.

Rispóndere, 67.

Ristáre, *see* stáre, 4.

Ródere, 52.

Rómpere, 134.

Salíre, 153.

Sapére, 6.

Scégliere, 86.

Scéndere, 53.

Scêrnere, 54.

Scérre, *see* scégliere, 86.

Scíndere, 76.

Sciôgliere, 87.

Sciôrre, *see* sciôgliere, 87.

Scomméttere, *see* méttere, 104.

Scopríre, *see* copríre, 138.

Scôrgere, 77.

Scrívere, 121.

Scuôtere, 112.

Sdrucíre, 148.

Sdruscíre, *see* sdrucíre, 148.

Sedére, 9.

Sedúrre, *see* condúrre, 123.

Seguíre, 146.

Seppellíre, 145.

Sêrpere (*defect.*): serpêndo; *Pres.*
sêrpo, sêrpi, sêrpe, sêrpono; *Imp.*
regular; Pres. Subj. sêrpa, sêrpano.

Silére (*defect.*): *Pres.* síli, síle.

Soffólcere (*defect.*): *Pres.* soffólce;
Pret. soffólse; *Past Part.* soffólto.

Soffcríre, *see* soffríre, 140.

Soffríre, 140.

Solére, 14.

Sôlvere, 135.

Sopprímere, *see* esprímere, 106.

Soprastáre, *see* stáre, 4.

Sórgere, 78.

Sospêndere, 55.

Sostáre, *is reg.*

Sottostáre, *see* stáre, 4.

Sovvertíre, *see* convertíre, 141.

Spándere, 79.

Spárgere, 56.

Sparíre, 151.

Spêgnere, 95.

Spêndere, 57.

Spôrgere, 58.

Spíngere, 96.

Spôrgere, 80.

Stáre, 4.

Strídere, *reg. verb, has no Past Part.*

Stríngere, 97.

Strúggere, 122.

Succêdere, 110.

Súggere, *reg. verb, has no Past Part.*

Sussístere, *see* esístere, 131.

Tacére, 13.

Tángere (*defect.*) : *Pres.* tánge.

Têndere (*trans.*), 59.

Têndere (*intrans.*), *reg. verb, has no
Past Part.*

Tenére, 17.

Têrgere, 60.

Tíngere, 98.

Tôgliere, 88.

Tôllere (*defect.*) : *Pres.* tôlli, tôlle ;
Pres. Subj. tôlla.

Tôrcere, 81.

Tôrpere (*defect.*) : *Pres.* tôrpo, tôrpi,
tôrpe, tôrpono ; *Pres. Subj.* tôrpa.

Tôrre, *see* tôgliere, 88.

Tradúrre, *see* condúrre, 123.

Tráere, *see* trárre, 124.

Trárre, 124.

Uccídere, 61.

Udíre, 155.

Úngere, 99.

Úrgere (*defect.*): *Pres.* úrge ; *Imp.*
urgéva, urgévano ; *Imp. Subj.* ur-
gésse, urgéssero.

Uscíre, 156.

Valére, 18.

Vedére, 10.

Vêllere, 100.

Veníre, 154.

Vêrre, *see* vêllere, 100.

Vígere (*defect.*) : *Pres.* víge; *Imp.*
vigéva.

Vilipêndere, *see* sospêndere, 55.

Víncere, 82.

Vívere, 136.

Volére, 19.

Vôlgere, 83.

ITALIAN-ENGLISH VOCABULARY.

A, to, at, in.
A', ái, al, *etc.* = a + *art.*
Abbellíto, beautified.
Accompagnáre, accompany.
Accôrgersi, perceive.
Ácqua, water.
Ad, *see* **A.**
Affacciársi, place one's self (*at a window*).
Affrettáre, hasten.
Agguantáre, seize.
Agostíno, Gus.
Álbero, tree.
Ále, wing.
Alétta, little wing.
Alettína, little wing.
Alfrédo, Alfred.
Allontanáre, send off.
Allóra, then.
Áltro, other.
Amáro, bitter.
Ánche, also, even.
Andár, *see* **Andáre.**
Andáre, go, to go, going.
Andársene, go away.
Andáto, gone.
Anêllo, ring.
Animále, animal.
Animalíno, little creature.
Antíco, old.
Ápe, bee.
Appéna, hardly.

Appôsta, on purpose.
Ária, air.
Arricchíto, enriched.
Arriváre, arrive.
Arriváto, having arrived.
Ásino, ass.
Assalíre, attack.
Assênzio, wormwood.
Assolúto, absolute.
Áttimo, flash.
Avánti a, in front of.
Avére, have.
Avvedérsi di, perceive.
Azionáccia, *from* **Azióne.**
Azióne, action.
Bábbo, father, papa.
Badáre, keep.
Bagnáre, bathe.
Bambíno, child.
Bárbaro, barbarian.
Barbóne, water-spaniel.
Baróne, baron.
Bastóne, stick.
Bel, *see* **Bêllo.**
Bellíssimo, very beautiful.
Bêllo, beautiful, fine, kind.
Ben, *see* **Bêne.**
Bêne, well, nicely, much.
Bêne, good (*noun*).
Bócca, mouth.
Bôve, ox.
Brávo, worthy.

Brilláre, shine.
Brútto, ugly.
Bucáto, pricked.
Bugía, lie.
Búio, dark.
Buôno, good.
Buttáre, throw.   *Buttár giù* = swallow.
Cadére, fall.
Calzóni, trousers.
Can, *see* Cáne.
Cáue, dog,
Capáce, capable.
Cápo, head.   *Da cápo, daccápo* = once more.
Cappêllo, hat.
Carlomágno, Charlemagne.
Cárne, flesh.
Cása, house, home.
Cascáre, fall.
Cassétta, drawer.
Cassettóne, bureau.
Castêllo, castle.
Cattívo, bad, naughty.
Cêlia, trick.
Cênto, a hundred.
Cercáre, search.
Cêrto, certain, some.
Cespúglio, bush.
Che, who, which, that.
Che, what.   *Che côsa* = what.
Che, that.
Che, than.
Chi . . . chi, one . . . another.
Chiamáre, call.
Chícca, sweetmeat.
Ci, there.
Cínque, five.

Città, city.
Cittadíno, citizen.
Côda, tail.
Côgli, col, *etc.* = cou + *art.*
Côgliere, catch, pick.
Côllo, neck.
Cóme, as, like, how, when.
Cominciáre, begin.
Comméttere, commit.
Compágno, companion.
Comúne, town.   *Comúni* = commons.
Cou, with.
Confêtti, candy.
Conóscere, know, find out.
Cónte, count.
Continovaménte, continually.
Contínuo, continual.
Cónto, count.
Côrpo, body.
Corrêggersi, reform.
Côsa, thing.   *Côsa púbblica* = government.
Così, so, thus.
Creatúra, creature.
Crédere, believe.
Cúi, whom, whose.
Curiosità, curiosity.
Curióso, curious, funny.
Da, by, from, as to.   *Dálle párti* = at the sides.
Daccápo, *see* Cápo.
Dái, dal, *etc.* = da + *art.*
Dáre, give, look.
De', dégli, déi, del, *etc.* = di + *art.*
Desidêrio, desire.
Détto, said, told.
Di, of, than, to, with.

Dicêrto, surely.
Di diêtro, from behind.
Diêci, ten.
Diêtro, behind, after. *Di diètro =* from behind. *Diètro a =* after.
Dintórni, neighborhood.
Dío, God.
Díre, say, speak.
Dirítto, right.
Discórso, talk.
Disobbediênte, disobedient.
Disperáto, desperate.
Distánza, distance.
Distrúggere, destroy.
Disubbidiênte, disobedient.
Ditíno, *from* Díto.
Díto, finger. *Dito grósso =* thumb.
Diventáre, become.
Dódici, twelve.
Dolóre, pain.
Dópo, after.
Dóve, where.
Dovére, ought, must.
Dúe, two.
Dúnque, therefore.
Duránte, during.
E, and.
Êcco, this is.
Ed, and.
Enríco, Henry.
Éssa, it.
Ésse, them.
Êssere, be. *Êssere per =* be about to.
Éssi, them.
Ésso, it.
Fállo, fault.
Fanciúllo, child.

Fáre, make, let.
Farfálla, butterfly.
Fasciáre, bandage.
Fêrro, iron.
Figliuôlo, child, son.
Figurársi, imagine.
Finchè non, until.
Finêstra, window.
Finíre, finish.
Fíno a, up to.
Fióre, flower.
Fioríto, flowery.
Firênze, Florence.
Firmaménto, firmament.
Fôglia, leaf.
Fónte, fountain.
Forestiêro, foreign.
Fra, between, in, to.
Fréddo, cold.
Frónte, forehead.
Frútto, fruit.
Fuggíre, flee.
Fuôri, out.
Fúria, haste.
Gámba, leg.
Gámbo, stem.
Gátto, cat.
Genitóri, parents.
Già, already.
Giardíno, garden.
Gíglio, lily.
Giorgétto, Georgie.
Giórno, day.
Girár, *see* Giráre.
Giráre, go around.
Giráto, gone around.
Gíro, turn, circuit.
Gíro gíro a, round and round.

Giù, down.
Giudízio, judgment, idea.
Gli, the.
Gli, it.
Gli, to him.
Glie, *see* Gli, Le.
Glôbo, globe.
Golóso, glutton, greedy.
Governáto, governed.
Gránde, big.
Grandíssimo, very big.
Grído, shout.
Grôsso, big.
Guardársi, refrain.
I, the.
Il, the.
Illumináto, illumined.
Il quále, who.
Imperatóre, emperor.
Impêro, empire.
In, in.
Infátti, in fact.
Infinitaménte, infinitely.
Infíno, even.
Infocáto, blazing.
Ingordígia, gluttony.
Insegnáre, teach.
Insêtto, insect.
Insiême, together.
Insómma, in short.
Intendiménto, intelligence.
Intórno, around (*adv.*).
Intórno a, around (*prep.*).
Invasióne, invasion.
Ispiráre, inspire.
L', *see* La, Le, Lo.
La, the.
La, it, her.

Là, there. *Di là* = there.
Laceráre, tear.
Ládra, thief.
Ládro, robber.
Lámpo, flash.
Lancétta, hand.
Lasciáre, leave, let, let go.
Lasciáto, let.
Lavoráre, work.
Le, the.
Le, to her, to it.
Le, them.
Leóne, lion.
Lêsto, quick.
Leváre, take away. *Levársi (with direct object)* = get rid of.
Leváto, up.
Li, them.
Lì, there.
Líbero, free.
Lo, the.
Lo, him, it.
Longobárdo, Longobard.
Lontáno, distant.
Lóro, them, their.
Lúce, light.
Lucêrtola, lizard.
Lúi, him, he.
Lúme, light.
Luminóso, luminous.
Lúna, moon.
Ma, but.
Mádre, mother.
Maestóso, majestic.
Maêstra, school-mistress.
Maêstro, school-master.
Mággio, May.
Maggióre, larger.

Mái, ever. *Non mái* = never.

Malánno, harm. *Far malánni* = mischief-making.

Maláta, ill.

Maldicênte, gossip.

Mále, badly, ill.

Mále, wicked.

Mámma, mother, mamma.

Mandáre, send.

Mangiáre, eat.

Maniêra, manner.

Máno, hand.

Mattína, morning.

Méno, less.

Ménto, chin.

Méntre, while.

Meraviglióso, wonderful.

Metà, half.

Méttere, put. *Méttersi* = begin, put on.

Mêzzo, half.

Mêzzo, middle. *In mêzzo a* = in the middle of.

Mício, puss, cat.

Milióne, million.

Minacciáre, threaten.

Minóre, smaller.

Minúto, minute.

Mío, my.

Môdo, way.

Molestáre, annoy.

Mólti, many.

Mólto, much.

Môrdere, bite.

Mósca, fly.

Móstra, face.

Múro, wall.

Mutáre, change.

Nascósto, hidden.

Náso, nose.

Náto, born.

Ne, of it, for it.

Nè, nor.

Néi, nel, *etc.* = in + *art.*

Nemméno, even.

Nessúno, nobody.

Niccolíno, Nicholas, Nick.

Nído, nest.

No, no. *Di no* = no.

Nôbile, noble.

Nobiltà, nobility.

Nói, we, us.

Nôia, trouble.

Non, not. *Non . . . che* = only.

Nôstro, our.

Nôtte, night.

Nôve, nine.

Núlla, nothing.

Número, number.

O, or.

O, oh.

Ôcchio, eye.

Occhióne, *from* Ôcchio.

Odóre, odor.

Ógni, every.

Ognúno, everybody.

Óltre, beyond, over.

Óra, now.

Óra, hour.

Oramái, at last.

Orígine, origin.

Òro, gold.

Orológio, watch.

Ôtto, eight.

Padroncíno, little master.

Palázzo, palace.

Panière, basket.
Panieríno, *from* Panière.
Pánni, clothes.
Parécchio, some.
Parére, seem.
Párte. part, side. *Dálle párti* = at the sides. *A quésta párte* = to this time.
Participáre, participate.
Pásso, step.
Pátto, condition. *A pátto che* = on condition that.
Pel = per il.
Pensáre, think.
Per, for, in order to, on account of, through, by.
Perchè, why, because.
Pêrdere, lose.
Perdonáre, pardon.
Permésso, permission.
Però, therefore, however.
Pésce, fish.
Pêtto, chest.
Piánta, plant.
Picchiáre, strike.
Piccíno, tiny, small.
Píccolo, little, small.
Piêde, foot.
Piêno, full.
Pigliáre, take.
Pínna, fin.
Più, more, most.
Po', little.
Pôi, then, too.
Portáre, take, bring.
Potére, can. be able.
Pôvero, poor.
Prêndere, take.

Prêsso, near.
Prêsto, early.
Pretêndere, expect.
Prevalére, prevail.
Prímo, first.
Prónto, quick.
Púbblico, public.
Puníre, punish.
Púnto, point.
Quadrúpede, quadruped.
Quálche, some.
Qualchedúno, somebody.
Qualcôsa, anything.
Qualcúno, somebody.
Quále, *see* Il quale.
Quándo, when.
Quánto, as much.
Quattórdici, fourteen.
Quáttro, four.
Que', quéi, *pl. of* Quéllo.
Quégli, *pl. of* Quéllo.
Quel, *see* Quéllo.
Quéllo, that.
Quésto, this.
Qui, here. *Di qui* = here.
Quíndi, therefore.
Raccontáre, relate.
Raggiúngere, overtake.
Ragióne, reason.
Rasênte, close.
Recreazióne, recess.
Refezióne, lunch.
Rêggere, stand, endure.
Respiráre, breathe.
Rêttile, reptile.
Riccárdo, Richard.
Ricominciáre, begin again.
Ricordársi, remember.

Rídere, laugh.

Ríga, line. *Di prima riga* = first-class.

Righettína, little mark.

Rimandáre, send back.

Rimanére, remain.

Rimediáre a, atone for.

Rimproveráre, reprove.

Ripêtere, repeat.

Ripôso, rest.

Rispóndere, reply.

Risputáre, spit again.

Rómpere, break.

Rôsa, rose.

Rotóndo, round.

Rubáre, steal.

Sanguinóso, bloody.

Sapére, know, hear.

Saporáccio, *from* Sapóre.

Sapóre, taste.

Sásso, stone.

Scappáre, run away.

Scêua, scene.

Scénder, *see* Scéndere.

Scéudere, descend.

Scuôla, school.

Se, if, whether.

Se, *see* Si.

Sè, itself, himself, herself.

Secóndo che, according as.

Seguáto, marked.

Seguíre, turn out.

Sêi, six.

Sêmpre, always.

Senése, Sienese.

Sentíre, taste, hear.

Sénza, without.

Sêrpe, snake.

Servitóre, servant.

Sessánta, sixty.

Sêtte, seven.

Sfacciatággine, impudence.

Si, himself, herself, itself.

Sì, yes, so.

Signóra, lady.

Siguóre, gentleman.

Siguoría, rule.

Símile, like.

Smisuráto, boundless.

Soáve, sweet.

Solaménte, only.

Sóle, sun.

Sollécito, early, brisk.

Sólo, alone.

Sommáto, added.

Sópra, on, above. *Di sópra* = up, above.

Sorêlla, sister.

Sorellína, *from* Sorêlla.

Sôrte, lucky.

Sospettáre, suspect.

Sospêtto, suspicion.

Sostégno, support.

Sótto, under. *Di sótto* = down, underneath.

Sparíre, disappear.

Spícchio, slice.

Spína, thorn.

Sputáre, spit.

Stáuza, room.

Stáre, stay, stand.

Stélla, star.

Stésso, himself.

Stésso, same.

Stésso, even.

Stracciáre, tear.

Strétto, close, tight.
Strillále, scream.
Su, on, up.
Su', sul, *etc.* = su + *art.*
Súbito, at once.
Súo, its, his, her.
Tánto, so much, so, much.
Tánto ... quánto, both ... and.
Te, thee, you.
Têmpo, time.
Tenúto, held. .
Têrra, earth, ground, land.
Territôrio, territory.
Ti, thee, you.
Tiráre, throw, draw. *Tirár fuôri,* take out.
Tócco, one o'clock.
Tornáre, return, returning.
Tórno tórno a, round and round.
Toscáno, Tuscan.
Tra, among. to.
Tranquillaménte, tranquilly.
Trátto : *a un trátto* = all at once.
Traversáre, cross.
Tre, three.
Trédici, thirteen.
Trónco, trunk.
Trováre, find.
Tu, thou, you.
Túo, thy, your.
Tútto, all. *Per tútto* = everywhere. *Tútti e dúe* = both ; *tútti e tre* = all three ; *etc.*
Uccellíno, *from* Uccêllo.
Uccêllo, bird.
Un, a, one.

Úna, a, one.
Úndici, eleven.
Úno, a, one.
Uôvo, egg.
Urláre, yell.
Úscio, door.
Vassoíno, tray.
Vedére, see.
Ventiquáttro, twenty-four.
Verità, truth.
Véro, true.
Véscovo, bishop.
Vêspa, wasp.
Vestíre, dress.
Vía, off, away, so forth. *Sometimes used instead of a verb of motion.*
Viággio, way, journey.
Vicíno, near.
Viôla, violet.
Viôttola, path.
Víso, face.
Víspo, lively.
Viziáccio, *from* Vízio.
Vízio, vice.
Vóce, voice.
Vôglia, desire.
Volére, wish.
Volontariaménte, voluntarily.
Vôlta, time.
Voltár, *see* Voltáre.
Voltáre, turn.
Zámpa, paw, foot.
Zampína, little paw.
Zanzára, mosquito.
Zimbêllo, laughing-stock.

ENGLISH-ITALIAN VOCABULARY.

A, un, úno, úna.
Africa, Áffrica.
After, dópo.
Ago, fa.
Aim, miráre.
Air, ária.
All, tútto.
Alone, sólo.
Although, sebbéne.
Always, sêmpre.
Amaze, meravigliáre.
America, América.
An, *see* A.
Ancient, antíco.
And, e.
Another, un áltro.
April, apríle, *m.*
Around, intórno.
As, cómc.
As . . . as, quánto, tánto . . . cóme.
Asia, Ásia.
At, a.
Attach, attaccáre.
August, agósto.
Be, éssere, *irreg.* (53, *a*).
Beam, tráve, *m. or f.*
Beast, béstia.
Beautiful, béllo.
Because, perchè.
Begin, cominciáre.
Believe, crédere.
Big, grôsso.

Bird, uccéllo.
Black, néro.
Blood, sángue, *m.*
Boil, bollíre.
Born, náto. *Pl.:* náti, *m.*; náte, *f.*
Boy, ragázzo.
Branch, rámo.
Bread, páne, *m.*
Brother, fratéllo, *m.*
Bubble, vescichétta.
But, ma.
By, da. *By chance* = per cáso.
Call, chiamáre.
Capital, capitále, *f.*
Car, vagóne, *m.*
Care, cúra.
Carriage, carrôzza.
Carry, portáre.
Case, cáso.
Ceiling, pálco.
Chance, cáso. *By chance* = per cáso.
Charged, cárico.
Charity, carità, *f.*
Charles, Cárlo.
Choose, scégliere. *irreg.*
Christopher, Cristóforo.
Circle, tóndo.
City, città, *f.*
Cloud, núvola.
Club, bastóne, *m.*
Coat, ábito.

Collect, raccôgliere, *irreg.*
Columbus, Colómbo.
Come back, tornáre.
Companion, compágno.
Confined, tenúto.
Construct, costruíre, *irreg.*
Continue, seguitáre.
Contrary, contrário.
Cool, raffreddársi.
Corner, cánto.
Country, paése, *m.*
Cover, copríre, *irreg.*
Creature, animále, *m.*
Crumb, bríciola.
Crush, schiacciáre.
Dark, búio.
Day, giórno.
December, dicêmbre, *m.*
Dense, dênso.
Department, dipartiménto.
Discover, scopríre, *irreg.*
Distance, distánza.
Divide, divídere, *irreg.*
Do, fáre, *irreg.*
Dominion, domínio.
Door, úscio.
Down, giù.
Dream, sognáre.
Drop, gócciola. *Drop by drop =*
a gócciola a gócciola.
Duke, dúca, *m.*
Dungeon, cárcere, *f.*
Dust, pólvere, *f.*
Earn, guadagnáre.
Earth, tèrra.
Eight hundred, ottocênto.
Eighty, ottánta.
Either ... or, o ... . o.

Emmanuel, Emmanuéle.
Emperor, imperatóre, *m.*
Empty, vuôto.
End, termináre.
Enemy, nemíco.
Escape, scappáre.
Europe, Europa.
Even, ánche.
Ever, mái.
Every, ógni.
Everything, tútto.
Everywhere, per tútto.
Eye, *noun*, ôcchio.
Eye, *vb.*, occhiáre.
Fall, cadúta.
Family, famíglia, *f.*
Far, lontáno.
Father, pádre, *m.*, bábbo.
February, febbráio.
Fief, fêudo.
Fifth, quínto.
Find, trováre.
Finger, díto. *Pl.* díta, *f.*
Fire, fuôco.
First, prímo. *Adv.*, príma.
Five, cínque.
Flat, piátto.
Flee, fuggíre.
Flower, fióre, *m.*
Fly, voláre.
Food, mangiáre, *m.*
For, per. *For yourself (conjunc-*
tive) = vi, si.
Form, formáre.
Fort, fortézza.
Forth, fuóri.
Forty, quaránta.
Four, quáttro.

Four hundred, quattrocénto.
France, Fráncia, *f.*
Friday, venerdì, *m.*
Friend, amíco, *m.*
From, da.
Fruit, frútto.
Furniture, mobília.
Genoa, Génova.
Give, dáre, *irreg.*
Go, andáre, *irreg.*
Good, buóno.
Grain, gráno.
Great, gránde.
Ground, térra.
Grove, boschétto.
Grow up, venír su, *irreg.*
Gun, schiôppo, fucíle, *m.*
Hand, máno, *f.*
Happen, accadére, *irreg.*
Hardly, appéna.
Hasten, affrettársi.
Hate, odiáre.
Have, avére, *irreg.* (53, *b*).
He, égli, lúi.
Heat, cáldo.
Her, la, le, léi.
Herb, érba.
Here, qua.
High, álto.
Him, lo, gli, lúi. *To him* = gli, a lúi.
Himself, si.
His, súo.
History, stôria.
Holiday, fésta.
Honest, onésto.
However, tuttavía.
Hunter, cacciatóre, *m.*

I, ío.
If, se.
Imagine, immagináre.
In, in.
Indeed, davvéro.
Inhabit, abitáre.
Inside, didéntro.
Instance, esémpio.
Intense, vívo.
Intention, intenzióne, *f.*
Into, in.
It, lo, la, égli, gli.
Italian, italiáno.
Italy, Itália, *f.*
Its, súo, súa.
Itself, si.
Jailer, carceriére, *m.*
January, gennáio.
July, lúglio.
June, giúgno.
King, re, *m.*
Know, sapére, *irreg.*, conóscere (= *be acquainted with*), *irreg.*
Land, paése, *m.*, térra.
Large, gránde.
Last, último (*precedes noun*).
Last year = l' ánno scórso.
Latter, quésto. *The latter* = quésti, *m. sing.*
Leaf, fóglia.
Leap-year, bisestíle, *m.*
Learn, imparáre.
Left, sinístra.
Lid, tésto.
Lift, solleváre.
Light, lúce, *f.*
Like, cóme.
Little (= *small*), píccolo, piccíno.

Little (= *a small quantity*). pôco.
Little by little = a pôco a pôco.
Live, vívere, *irreg.*
Loaded, cárico.
Lorraine : *of Lorraine*=lorenése.
Loud, fôrte.
Low, básso.
Lower, abbassáre.
Man, uômo, *pl.* uômini.
Many, môlti, *m.*, môlte, *f.*
March, márzo.
Mask, máschera.
May, mággio.
Me, mi, me.
Melon, cocômero.
Merchant, mercánte, *m.*
Middle, mézzo.
Mignonette, amoríno.
Mine, mío.
Moisture, umidità, *f.*
Monday, lunedì, *m.*
Month, mése, *m.*
Moon, lúna.
More, più.
Mortify, mortificáre.
Most, il più.
Mr., signór.
My, mío.
Name, nóme, *m.*
Napoleon, Napoleóne.
Near, vicíno a.
Need, bisógno.
Never, non . . . mái.
Nice, gentíle.
Ninety, novánta.
No, no.
Nobody, nessúno.
Nor, nè.

Not, non.
November, novêmbre.
Now, óra.
Object, oggêtto.
Observe, osserváre.
Oceanica, Oceánia.
October, ottóbre.
Of, di. *Of them* = ne.
On, sópra, su (*before vow.*, sur).
One, úno.
One's self, si.
Only, sólo (*adj.*), non . . . che
    (*adv.*).
Opposite, oppósto.
Or, o.
Other, áltro.
Ought, dovére, *irreg.*
Out, fuôri.
Outside, difuôri, *m.*
Over there, laggiù.
Pace, pásso.
Parents, genitóri, *m. pl.*
Paris, Parígi.
Parrot, pappagállo.
Part, párte, *f.*
Peasant, contadíno.
Perfectly, prôprio.
Perhaps, fórse.
Persuade, persuadére, *irreg.*
Philip, Filíppo.
Place, luôgo.
Placed, pósto.
Plainly, schiettaménte.
Plant, piánta.
Point, púnto.
Poor, pôvero.
Pot, péntola.
Present, presentáre.

Prevent, impedíre.
Principle, princípio.
Prison, prigióne, *f.*
Prisoner, prigioniéro.
Profession, professióne, *f.*
Purpose, úso.
Quantity, quantità, *f.*
Question, dománda.
Rain, pióggia.
Raise, leváre.
Rare, ráro.
Recognized, conosciúto.
Relate, raccontáre.
Remain, rimanére, *irreg.*, restáre.
Repeat, ripétere.
Reply, rispóndere, *irreg.*
Resolve, risciógliere, *irreg.*
Rest, posáre.
Right, déstra.
Rise, salíre, *irreg.*
Room, stánza.
Root, radíce, *f.*
Round, rotóndo.
Rule, signoría. ·
Sacrifice, sacrifízio.
Sail, navigáre.
Sailor, marináro.
Same, stésso (*precedes noun*).
Satisfy, contentáre.
Saturday, sábato.
Say, díre, *irreg.*
Sea, máre. *m.*
Second, secóndo.
See, vedére, *irreg.*
Seed, séme, *m.*
Sent, mandáto.
September, settémbre, *m.*
Service, servízio.

Seven, sétte.
Shake, scuótere, *irreg.*
Ship, náve, *f.*
Shoot, bárba.
Short, córto.
Show off, far vedére, *irreg.*
Side, párte, *f.*
Silence, siénzio.
Sinister, sinístro.
Sir, signóre, *m.*
Sixty, sessánta.
Sky, ciélo.
Small, píccolo, piccíno.
Smoke, fúmo.
So, così.
So as to, per.
Some, quálche.
Somebody else, qualchedun' ál-
tro.
Sometimes, qualchevólta.
So much, tánto.
Son, fíglio.
Sort, sórta.
Spaniard, spagnuólo.
Speak, parláre.
Spider, rágno, rágnolo.
Sprouted, germogliáto.
Stalk, fústo.
Star, stélla.
Steam, vapóre, *m.*
Straight, dirítto.
Study, *noun*, stúdio.
Study, *vb.*, studiáre.
Sun, sóle, *m.*
Sunday, doménica.
Support, mantenére, *irreg.*
Surprised, sorpréso.
Surround, circondáre.

Table, távola.
Take, prêndere, *irreg.*
Tear, raschiáre.
Than, che, di.
Thanks, grázie, *f. pl.*
That, *conj.*, che.
That, *rel. pron.*, che.
That, *demons. pron.*, quéllo.
The, il, lo, la, i, gli, le.
Them, li, le, lóro.   *Of them* = ne.
Then, pôi.
There, là, lì.
Therefore, però.
They. éssi, ésse, lóro.
Thick, grôsso.
Thing, côsa.
Think, pensáre.
Third, têrzo.
Thirtieth, trentêsimo.
Thirty, trénta.
Thirty-first, trentêsimo prímo.
Thirty-one, trentúno, trentún.
This, quésto.
Thousand, mílle.
Three, tre.
Three hundred, trecênto.
Thursday, giovedì, *m.*
Thus, così.
Time, vôlta, têmpo. *Another time use* vôlta.
To, a.   *To him* = gli.
Together, insiême.
Too (= *also*), ánche.
Too (= *excessively*), trôppo.
Tree, álbero.
Trunk, trónco.
Tuesday, martedì, *m.*
Turn, giráre.

Tuscan, toscáno.
Twelve, dódici.
Twenty-eight, ventôtto.
Twenty-nine, ventinôve.
Twig, ramoscéllo.
Two, dúe.
Under, sótto.
Unfortunate, infelíce.
Unhappy, sventuráto.
Union, unióne, *f.*
Unite, raccôgliere, *irreg.*
Until, *prep.*, fíno a.
Until, *conj.*, finchè . . . non.
Us, nói, ci (*conjunctive*).
Usual, usáto.
Vapor, vapóre, *m.*
Vegetable, vegetábile, *m.*
Very, mólto, tánto.
Victor, Vittôrio.
Villa, vílla.
Village, villággio.
Water, ácqua.
Way (= *manner*), maniêra.
We, nói.
Web, téla.
Wednesday, mercoledì, *m.*
Week, settimána.
What, *interrog. and exclam.*, che.
What, *rel.*, quéllo che.
When, quándo.
Where, dóve.
Which, che.
While, méntre.
Who, *rel.*, che.
Whom, *rel.*, cúi.
Willingly, volentiêri.
Wind, vênto.

Window, finêstra.
With, con.
Without, sénza.
Wood, bósco.
Word, parôla.
Working-day, giórno di lavóro.
World, móndo.

Year, ánno.
Yes, già.
You, vói, vi, Lêi, la, le. *To you*
= vi, le.
Your, vôstro, Súo.
Yourself, vi, si. *For yourself =*
vi, si.

INDEX.